10-13

W9-BDK-912

ANYWHERE BUT HERE

ANYWHERE BUT HERE

TANYA LLOYD KYI

Simon Pulse

New York   London   Toronto   Sydney   New Delhi

SIMON PULSE

An imprint of Simon & Schuster Children's Publishing Division

1230 Avenue of the Americas, New York, NY 10020

First Simon Pulse edition October 2013

Text copyright © 2013 by Tanya Kyi

Cover photograph copyright © 2013 by plainpicture/Pierre Baelen

All rights reserved, including the right of reproduction in whole or in part in any form.

SIMON PULSE and colophon are registered trademarks of Simon & Schuster, Inc.

For information about special discounts for bulk purchases, please contact Simon & Schuster Special Sales at 1-866-506-1949 or business@simonandschuster.com.

The Simon & Schuster Speakers Bureau can bring authors to your live event. For more information or to book an event contact the Simon & Schuster Speakers Bureau at 1-866-248-3049 or visit our website at www.simonspeakers.com.

Book design by Karina Granda

The text of this book was set in Adobe Garamond Pro.

Manufactured in the United States of America

2 4 6 8 10 9 7 5 3 1

Library of Congress Cataloging-in-Publication Data

Kyi, Tanya Lloyd, 1973–

Anywhere but here / Tanya Lloyd Kyi. — First Simon Pulse edition.

p. cm.

Summary: Ever since his mom died, Cole feels stuck. He just wants to graduate and leave his small, suffocating town. And everything is going according to plan—until Cole discovers the one secret that could keep him there . . . forever.

[1. Coming of age—Fiction. 2. Grief—Fiction. 3. Interpersonal relations—Fiction.

4. Documentary films—Production and direction—Fiction.

5. Single-parent families—Fiction. 6. Canada—Fiction.] I. Title.

PZ7.K9795Any 2013   [Fic]—dc23   2012051439

ISBN 978-1-4424-8070-4 (hc)

ISBN 978-1-4424-8069-8 (pbk)

ISBN 978-1-4424-8071-1 (eBook)

YA KYI

For Min, Julia, and Matthew

chapter 1

misguided dreams that interfere with perfectly hungover sleep

The first time I wake up, I lie there wondering what day it is. I can see sunlight poking through the curtains, high on the cement wall of my basement bedroom.

I roll over to look at the clock: 9:54.

Shit! Shit, shit, shit! I leap out of bed as if the mattress has caught fire and grab my pants off the floor. It's Friday, and Lauren hasn't called to wake me up because Lauren isn't my girlfriend anymore, and calling lazy-ass guys to cajole them to school is no longer in her job description.

A minute later I'm back on the bed. Perched with my head in my hands, dry heaving, I wish I'd called Greg last night instead of hanging out with Dallas. Dallas had an unfortunately generous beer supply. And the pants I just pulled on smell distinctly of vomit.

I wonder if I puked before or after leaving his house. Hopefully after. Then I wonder what my statistical chances are of passing next week's history final if I don't go to the review class this morning.

I roll my eyes toward the ceiling.

Battle of the Plains of Abraham . . . 1759.

Leader of the French . . . Montcalm.

Leader of the English . . . Wolfe.

Winner . . . must have been the English.

Importance of the Plains of Abraham . . . no freaking idea.

But I'm going to pass, no problem. I yank the pants off again, crawl under the covers, and go back to sleep.

I wake for the second time in the early afternoon, stagger to the bathroom for two Tylenol and a drink from the faucet, then flop back onto my mattress. My book flies from where it was balanced on top of my headboard and almost brains me. *The Guerilla Film Makers Handbook*, by Chris Jones and Genevieve Jolliffe. One day, I'm going to make documentaries the way some of the people in this book make films.

Not today, though.

There's a pounding at the basement door. It's probably only

a tapping, but in my booze-addled cranium, it echoes.

I stagger over and fling it open. "What?"

I'm still in my boxers. I wouldn't notice except that Lauren is standing in the carport looking like the leggy blonde from a romantic comedy, wearing a bright red dress and movie-star sunglasses.

"You look nice," I mumble.

"You look awful, Cole," she says, slipping off the glasses. "Can I come in?"

Can my ex-girlfriend come in? She doesn't *look* dangerous. As long as she doesn't yell, I should be able to survive this. Our first, awkward, post-breakup conversation has to happen sometime, right?

I move aside. Waving good-bye to her friend Lex, who's loitering on the sidewalk, Lauren sweeps past me through the hall and into my room, a wisp of vanilla perfume in her wake. She smells like a birthday cake fresh from the oven.

I follow her in and sit on my desk chair, crossing my arms and trying to look as if I have it together.

"Gross," she says. "It's like something died in here." Without asking, she opens my window.

"How was school?" I'm hunting for a safe topic of conversation. It's strange how you can talk to someone almost every day for two years and then feel suddenly so . . . separate.

"You missed the review session," she says. Lauren is the most dedicated student I know. If the town of Webster were attacked by *Shaun of the Dead* zombies, Lauren would take her textbooks into hiding with her.

She's good at commitment.

"What exactly did you do last night?" She picks up my jeans between her thumb and her forefinger and carries them to the hamper like toxic waste before straightening the quilt on my bed.

"Since when are you my mother?" I yawn.

I say it without thinking, but Lauren freezes.

"Sorry," she says.

I shrug. "I didn't mean it that way."

"I don't want to make you think about your mom."

"Really, it's okay."

"I don't want to bicker with you, either. I came over because last night, with my mom hovering in the kitchen, I felt like we didn't get a chance to talk properly, and . . ."

"Sure."

But just so we don't have to discuss things right this second, I leave to find my toothbrush.

The third time I wake up, Lauren's leg is thrown over mine. And it's naked. This is another good thing about Lauren. You wouldn't think that an honor roll student with the work ethic of John Ford and a religious fanatic for a mother would be willing to sleep with me. She always said it was okay because we'd been together forever and because we were going to be . . .

"Mmmmm," she breathes, wiggling closer and brushing her fingertips across my chest. She looks up at me with those blue eyes that seem brighter when she's happy. "I'm so glad we're okay again."

My whole body tenses. I try to smile, but I can feel it turning into a grimace.

"What?" she says. She's like that. She picks up my feelings through my skin, using weird lizard senses.

"I . . . um . . ." I don't get any farther than that. There are too many things going on inside my head, and none of them are good. Potential sentences are swirling together like water in a toilet bowl. Did I say we were getting back together? I didn't. I'm hungover, not wasted. I definitely did not say we were getting back together. I *did* just sleep with her. And I'm not such a jerk that I can sleep with her and then shove her out of bed.

I could run.

"Oh, yikes!" I've never said "yikes" in my life, but that's what comes out. "It's four o'clock already? I have to be at the school. Guidance counselor. I gotta run."

I pull on my jeans—clean ones—while I spout some

nonsense about not wanting to miss the college application talk. It's true that I have an appointment. We all automatically get one so we can talk about The Future before choosing our senior classes. Everyone knows the counselors spout a load of bunk. If they actually knew anything about the future, they wouldn't be working as part-time high school fake-a-shrinks, would they?

I'd planned to blow off the appointment. Now, suddenly, it seems extremely convenient to go.

Lauren makes sounds in her throat as if she would like to talk, but I don't even look at her. I tug on a T-shirt, grab my house keys from my dresser, and bolt.

"You might have to get dressed. Dad will be home from work in a while. I'll see you soon," I tell her as I dash toward the door.

I jog the first couple blocks down the hill, just in case she calls after me.

chapter 2

false fronts and uninvited counseling

What was I thinking? I don't even want to consider the emotional mess I've caused. What I'd like to do—and so far, this is my best idea of the day—is to pretend it never happened.

Never happened.

I head toward Canyon Street. Just as I get there, the sun comes out from behind a patch of clouds, and I force myself to take a deep breath and look around.

Normal. I'm going to act as normal as the other people meandering down the street.

This is where I would start if I were making a documentary about Webster. I wouldn't open with the tourism brochure approach: wildlife refuge, lakeshore, and hang glider takeoff points. Those are scenic and all, but how many people hang glide?

No, I would fade in like this:

> [Setting: *Canyon Street, town's main drag. Old brick bank visible in distance. Street is lined with false-fronted stores, suitable for a Wild West movie.*]

Even though the shops along here are box shaped, each has a tall front wall of a different color, decorated in carved gingerbread-style wood or hung with an old-fashioned sign. The style must have been all the rage when Canyon Street was built. To me, it makes Webster look like something created by a set designer and built inside a soundstage.

I'm just about to turn toward the school when one of our senior-citizen neighbors spots me.

"How are things going for you and your dad, Cole?"

They always ask the same questions, and they always have the same sympathetic look in their eyes.

"Great," I say. "Everything's going great!"

In the last twenty-four hours, I got hammered with Dallas, then screwed my ex-girlfriend, and now I have to see a counselor. Yup, it's going great.

"Late for an appointment, though!"

I turn downhill again. If this town is a Wild West set, the high school is something else entirely—a square, white, cinder-block building. So white that if it didn't say WEBSTER HIGH in big block letters, you'd think surgeons with sterile scalpels might be practicing lobotomies just inside.

I push through the double doors and into the tiled foyer, where my footsteps echo. It's 4:05, and everyone's cleared out. There's only the receptionist sitting at her massive desk with her one-hundred-button phone, and teachers' voices from the staff room behind her, and the ricocheting sounds of basketball practice from the gym.

Down the hall in the glassed-in waiting area of the counselors' offices, I flop onto a chair. A few minutes later, Ms. Gladwell swings her door open and sends the last student back into the world.

"You can call me *anytime* if you ever need *anything*," she says. It's obvious the pipsqueak who's leaving doesn't believe her. No one ever does.

"Come in, Cole. Grab a seat," she says, motioning to the gray swivel chair that passes for a black couch in her office.

I'm assigned to the worst counselor in the school. She's new, for one thing. Apparently, she moved here from the coast last year because her doctor recommended a dry climate for her asthma. She looks like she has asthma. She looks like an asthmatic mouse

with severe cheese allergies. And maybe a thyroid problem. She has stringy yellow hair, huge glasses, and even though she weighs about as much as my forearm, she dresses in men's gray T-shirts. Anyone can see that she's the one who needs counseling.

"So," she chirps. "We have to figure out what you're going to do next year. Any ideas?"

I shrug. I have ideas, but the thought of talking to her about them seems as appealing as a trip to the dentist. I pause to mentally curse Lauren for chasing me out of my own house and landing me here. Now that I think about it, this whole appointment is exactly like a trip to the dentist. All that's missing is the smell of fluoride and the sound of suction.

Fifteen minutes. I only have to live through fifteen minutes, and then I can go home. Lauren will be gone. It will be like it never happened.

Ms. Gladwell fans a few catalogs on the low, round table between us. They're for Purcell Technical, the College of the Rockies, and a vocational school in Calgary. Apparently, Ms. Gladwell doesn't think much of my academic potential.

"You think I'm going to be a plumber?"

She blinks. "These schools offer a lot more than plumbing programs. Besides, there's nothing wrong with being a plumber. Good money."

"I was thinking of something . . . farther away." Like, if this

office were Mercury and my future school were on one of the moons of Pluto. That would be perfect.

"Oh. I see," Ms. Gladwell says brightly after she's rustled through my file for a while. She pushes her glasses farther up her nose and gathers the first batch of catalogs. "So you're headed to university, then. What are you thinking of studying? There are good history grades here." She taps my file with a chewed fingernail.

"I was thinking film."

I clamp my jaw shut. How did that get out? I mean, I *was* thinking it, but I must be losing my mind to share something like that with Ms. Gladwell. It's as good as saying I'm going to be a performance artist or an astronaut. It's just not something that happens for regular people, especially not people from a small town like Webster. The population of serious doc fans in this high school is probably one: me.

Damn Lauren for turning my head inside out today.

Grimacing, I tug the front of my hair and spin in the chair a bit. At this rate, I'm going to end up in a nuthouse, not a frat house.

"That's wonderful," Ms. Gladwell says. She's smiling. Maybe she really does think it's wonderful. At least it's different. She probably listens to ten kids a day tell her they're going to be farmers or loggers. Greg wants to be a mechanic. I know Dallas will get a job on the pipeline with his dad. And Lauren has some sort of teacher/mom-of-the-year dream job in mind.

My friends call Webster "the Web," which is fitting. The town traps people like a giant spiderweb. They get married, get jobs at the mill, and pretty soon they have wrinkles and curved shoulders and are on the waiting list for the Blossom Valley Retirement Home.

Turning away from me, Ms. Gladwell rummages in a big black filing cabinet. "I have a catalog here for you. I know they sent me some. I haven't had anyone ask, but I thought maybe some of the drama students—ah! Here's one!"

Waving it in the air as if she's found the answer to all my problems, Ms. Gladwell steps toward me—and trips on the wheeled leg of her chair.

It's strange how things can happen in slow motion and in double speed, simultaneously. In slow-mo, her toe catches on the chair leg and her body arcs forward, the pamphlet flying out of her hand like a paper airplane.

In skip frame, without thinking, I stand up and catch her. Her chest hits mine and her head lands on my shoulder. She's as light as she looks. It's like hugging a child.

When Dallas swings open the office door with a cheerful "Howdy," that's how he finds us. Me with my arms wrapped around Ms. Gladwell, her hair brushing my neck and her breasts pressed against me.

He stops, his smile frozen on his freckled face. "I'll wait for y'all outside," he says.

The door closes.

"Damn," Ms. Gladwell and I say at exactly the same time. Then, as she scrambles to compose herself and I pretend I didn't notice her breasts touching me, we start to laugh. Obviously, Dallas won't be able to resist describing this scene. Tomorrow, the whole school will hear about Cole Owens making out with the counselor in her office. We both know it's going to be excruciatingly embarrassing for the next forty-eight-hour Webster High gossip cycle, and there's something funny about the situation.

"I'm such a klutz. Sorry about that," she says.

"No worries. But I'm gonna go."

"It might be best."

I try to look nonchalant as I pass Dallas in the hall, but he gives me a "you dog" kind of grin. It's definitely going to be all over school tomorrow.

"Cole? Cole?"

My shoulders tense. Is she crazy? Why is she calling after me?

When I turn, Ms. Gladwell hurries from the outer office into the hallway, her hair still mussed as if we *did* just make out. She's waving the film school pamphlet in her hand.

"Don't forget this."

"Sure. Cool. Thanks, Ms. Gladwell."

"Thanks, Ms. Gladwell." Dallas's falsetto, mimicking me, follows me into the foyer and out the door.

It's no big deal, I tell myself. This is just one more opportunity to implement my new life strategy: Concentrate on the future. Pretend the past never happened.

chapter 3

how to tell when something's done

Our house has smelled different this year, since Mom died. It's
not that I miss her perfume. I don't even think she wore perfume.
No, it's more that the house has taken on a sort of mildewed, dirty
laundry smell. If you wore a sweat sock, then dipped the toe in
beer and stuffed it under the carpet in the middle of your living
room, leaving it there for a few hot, almost-summer days, people
wouldn't necessarily know where to look, but they'd know that
something wasn't right. That's the kind of smell I mean.

I used to come home and smell dinner, not the frozen pizzas that Dad and I throw in the oven. Not "some damn decent
guy food, Cole," as Dad calls it. I mean real dinner, like roast
chicken.

On the Sunday after my accidental post-breakup sex scene, I start thinking. *Making real food can't be* that *hard*. If I'm going to focus only on the future, I'd like my future to include meals. And Sunday's when people are supposed to have family dinners, right?

Dad's nowhere to be found, so I grab his pickup keys off the kitchen table and drive down to the grocery store.

I do pretty well, at first. I find a bag of carrots and some tiny potatoes—the kind with the flaky skins. Then I hit the meat section. The chickens squat there wrapped in plastic like bald, alien life-forms. Scenes from *Food, Inc.* start scrolling through my mind. Factory farms and slaughterhouses and birds so top-heavy they can't walk . . .

"Whatcha lookin' for, hon?" A woman nudges her cart alongside mine. She looks like an aging diva with big blond hair, dangling silver earrings, and enough turquoise eye shadow to paint a house.

"I wanted to roast a chicken."

"You gonna make it yourself? Special occasion? That's real sweet."

"Thanks. I, um . . . don't really know how, though."

As the woman leans against her grocery cart, her breasts hang all the way down to the handle. I try to focus on her face. She has a nice person's eyes. I'll bet she's one of those people who can make little kids laugh.

"It's real easy, hon. You wash that bird under cold water—inside and out, mind—then pop it in a pan and rub it with oil and salt. Put your potatoes and veggies around the bottom. Half an hour at four hundred, then maybe two hours at three twenty-five. You got that?"

"Half an hour at four hundred, then two at three twenty-five," I repeat.

"Wiggle the leg around when you think it's cooked. If it feels like it's gonna fall right off, you've done good."

When I get home, I do exactly as she said. I wash the thing, I dig out the bag of guts and toss it in the garbage, and then I smear the bird with oil. She didn't say whether to cover it or not, so I leave the lid off the pan and hope for the best.

Once the chicken's been in the oven for an hour, the whole house starts to smell like Christmas in June. I sit on the couch in the living room waiting for the timer to buzz, my mouth watering.

Just in time, I hear Dad stomp in the front door and grunt as he pulls off his boots on the landing. He comes into the living room like a bloodhound on the scent of a body. I can actually see him sniffing. He's a big guy, built like a wrestler. At the lumberyard, I've seen him heave boards as if they're toothpicks.

"The neighbors bring somethin' by, Cole?" he asks. For a couple weeks last summer, right after Mom's funeral, the neighbors left casseroles on our front stoop every night. Only for a couple weeks, though.

"I cooked." I try to sound casual.

Dad's eyebrows shoot up, and he goes straight to the kitchen to investigate. "Looks done," he calls. "You going to carve?"

He's using his hearty voice, which is fake enough for reality TV. Dad alternates between sessions of complete immobility on the couch and sessions of pretending everything's perfect. I'm pretty sure the latter are for my sake.

I shrug from the doorway. "You can carve."

"No, no. You should try." Dad pulls out a cutting board and a knife. He waves the blade to motion me over, then he shows me how to twist off the wings and slice into the breast meat.

"That's some good chicken," he says once we're sitting at the kitchen table. It *is* good. The skin's nice and crisp, and the meat . . . well, it tastes more like meat than the pepperoni on frozen pizzas does.

After that—after we both finish saying how good it is—we run out of things to talk about. I glance at Dad now and then, watching the glow of the kitchen light reflect off the dome of his head, noticing the squint lines around his eyes. He glances at me, noticing . . . I have no idea what. I don't know what we're doing sitting at the kitchen table, anyway. Dad and I always eat in the living room.

"Want to turn on the TV?" I ask finally when there are only smears left on our plates.

"May as well," he says.

There's nothing left of the chicken. We scrape the bones into the trash and stick the roasting pan in the dishwasher. Add two plates. Two sets of silverware. When we flick off the kitchen lights, it's as if dinner never happened.

Then we crash on the couch and watch World War I repeat itself on the History Channel. Everything and everyone coated in gore and mud.

Later that night, when the dishes are done and Dad's snoring on the couch, I find myself roaming the house. I flick on the TV again, then turn it off. I pick up a book, but I can't concentrate.

I feel like bawling in a way I haven't cried since I was probably three years old. I miss Mom so bad it's as if someone has cut through my chest with a chain saw.

It's not just because of the chicken, either.

Usually, at a time like this, I would call Lauren. She'd come over for a while, or I'd pick her up in Dad's truck.

Once last year, after we'd heard bad news from the doctor's office, I couldn't handle staying in the house anymore. I didn't want to hear Mom say, "We just have to take it one day at a time," or Dad say, "Those doctors don't realize how tough you are."

That night, I picked up Lauren and we went to the park and sat on the swings. She didn't ask any questions. And then we were swinging. When you're as big as me and you swing on kids' playground equipment, it feels as if you're going to lift the entire metal frame from the ground and soar out into space.

It feels good.

Calling Lauren's not an option anymore, though. I slip outside and walk down the hill to Greg's house instead.

By the time I get there, it's too late to ring the doorbell. I bang on his bedroom window. Greg's family lives in one of the 1950s bungalows that line most of Webster's streets. They're perfectly rectangular, with windows all the same size, like a picture drawn by a little kid. Greg's has stucco on the top half and then a stripe of orange boards, then more stucco. It's butt ugly, actually.

Greg's twelve-year-old sister turns on her light and squints outside. I wave. She sends her eyes skyward, a perfect little copy of her mother, and flicks her light off.

When Greg finally pokes his head out, his brown hair is sticking straight up. There's a red crease on his cheek where it's been squished against the pillow.

"This better be good," he says.

"It is. It is," I assure him. "I've come to celebrate the freedom of man. This man, in particular. You are looking at a newly single Cole Owens. Bring out the girls and let's have a toast!"

"I have no girls," he grumbles. "And you have no drinks."

Then the rest of my words slowly worm their way into his sleep-dulled head. "You and Lauren broke up? Are you serious?"

"Serious as a train wreck," I say. "Now get out here. And bring something to drink."

A few minutes later Greg emerges with a bottle of rye and an extra jacket.

"That's why you're my best friend," I tell him after an hour of committed drinking. I flip over from where I've been sprawled on the community center field to slug Greg on the shoulder. Blades of grass stick to me. The ground is still spongelike from the spring rain, and I can smell the dirt clinging to my hair. "How many guys would get up in the middle of the night, provide alcohol, *and* think to bring me a jacket? You're quality, man. Quality."

"Yeah, right. And you're drunk," he says. "So how come Lauren dumped you, anyway?"

"She didn't dump me."

He looks doubtful. "Who started the conversation?"

"I did!" I'm forging into the future here. Deciding my own destiny. I thought this would be more obvious.

"What the hell were you thinking?"

"What do you mean, what was I thinking? For months I've been telling you that things aren't the same."

He nods. "I just figured . . ."

"You figured what?"

"I figured you were still feeling down about your mom. I thought you'd get through it."

Get through it. Is that what I'm supposed to do? I can't ask. My voice will come out wrong.

"Nope," I say instead. "Time for a change."

Greg rubs his forehead. I know what he expected. Lauren and I would keep dating and eventually get married, buy a house, then hatch mini-Coles. Everybody thought that. I'm screwing with an entire town's worldview right now.

There's a pause in the conversation while I pick hunks of grass from the field and take a good look at Greg. He isn't as big as me, but he's wiry. He no longer has the round cheeks from our kindergarten monkey-bar days. In fact, as I peer at him in the dim glow from the community center's streetlights, he looks almost exactly like his dad. Under his farm-boy mop of hair, he has the same round brown eyes and broad nose—even the same cleft in his chin. I wonder if he's going to stay in town like his dad, take over the auto shop, spend his spare time overhauling that RX-7 he's so proud of. Maybe he will.

He obviously thinks I'm making a mistake with Lauren, and that irritates me. I try to think of a way to explain.

I admit, Lauren's great. She's one of the sweetest people

I've ever met, in that can't-pass-a-dog-without-petting-it kind of way. Once, we'd driven a few hours to the mall in Spokane, and there was this old woman at the top of the escalator, frozen. Her daughter was at the bottom.

"Just grab the rail and step, Mom," the daughter was saying, a note of exasperation in her voice.

The mom put a toe forward toward the stair, tottered slightly, and slid her foot back to safety.

Before I'd even absorbed the situation, Lauren walked right up to that old lady, took her elbow, and stepped with her onto the escalator.

That's the kind of nice I mean.

But nice isn't everything.

"Remember last month when there was a partial eclipse, some sliver of the moon that wasn't going to look that way for another six centuries or something?"

Greg nods.

"Well, I borrowed the truck and I stuffed all the blankets from my bed into the back so we could lie there and look straight up. But when I got to Lauren's, she'd fallen asleep and she was too tired to go out."

Greg stares at me blankly. I haven't explained things well enough.

"Wait. I have a better example. We watched a documentary

one night about child soldiers in Uganda, and I said I would love to go and make films about stuff like that. Lauren rolled her eyes and said, 'We don't even know where Uganda is.'"

I don't tell Greg what she said next: that I shouldn't make life plans during my time of grief. Who says that? What kind of person under the age of forty says "time of grief"?

Greg still doesn't get it.

"Listen, maybe I won't ever go to Uganda. Maybe I don't know exactly where it is in Africa. But I don't want my girlfriend assuming we can't get there. I want her to feel like we're going to go wherever the hell we want for the rest of our lives. Isn't that how it should be?"

By this time I'm yelling and a dog is barking nearby and Greg's agreeing with me, probably to make me shut up.

Things get sloppy after that. At one point I pin Greg on the grass and force him to tell me that I've made the right decision about breaking up with Lauren. Then I sling my arm around his shoulders on the way back to his house and tell him that he's the best damn guy in the whole town.

He drives me home.

"If you had to break up, you picked the right time," he says as we wind through empty streets.

"Why's that?"

"Way I see it, this is going to be the best summer of our lives.

Next year we're getting ready to graduate. Everyone's going to be stressing over college applications, or getting jobs, or looking for jobs. We're facing serious stuff in one year, man. This is the last summer of freedom. The countdown's on."

I think that's the most apocalyptic view of life I've ever heard. I would say so, if I were up to pronouncing "apocalyptic."

"Besides," Greg continues with a grin. "Hannah Deprez is hot for you."

My face flushes in the darkness of the car. "Hannah? She is?"

Now that would be different. And different . . . it's a good thing, right? Greg can consider this his last summer of freedom if he wants to. I'm going to think of it as the first year of change.

chapter 4

close encounters of the warped mind

I'm whistling as I unlock the basement door and chuck my pack into a corner, where it can stay for the next two months. My exams are finished, my report card's collected, and I have all summer to celebrate.

I yell a hello and head upstairs.

No one's home. I can tell Dad stopped here after work—his stuff upstairs is tossed around the same way mine is downstairs. He's gone out, though, and the house is cold and silent.

My mom was a quiet person, but the quiet when people are in the house together is different from the empty kind. As I make myself some peanut-butter-and-jam sandwiches, I try to imagine she's here in the kitchen with me.

She always had to stand on her tiptoes to see over my shoulder.

"You eat that, you'll ruin your dinner," she'd say. Since we both knew that I could eat a stack of sandwiches and every other scrap of food in the fridge and still be hungry, she'd say it as a what-moms-are-supposed-to-say sort of thing.

When I took the milk out of the fridge, she'd hand me a glass so I wouldn't drink out of the jug. Then I'd lean against the counter to eat and she'd stand nearby slicing onions on the plastic cutting board, looking at the knife and the onions but really paying attention to me.

"I'm going to work a few shifts at the cherry plant this summer," I'd tell her. "I just finished exams. And I broke up with Lauren."

"The cherry plant sounds good. Hard work, though. You and Lauren broke up?" Her voice would be neutral. She wasn't one of those people who would tell you there were other fish in the sea. And she wasn't someone who would list all the things she hated about your ex, as if that would make you feel better. She was smarter than that.

"You doing okay?" she'd ask, scraping the onions and some tomatoes into a pan.

"Yeah. I think Lauren's still upset." Understatement. There was one enormously awkward phone call after the sex incident, and she hasn't spoken to me since.

It takes me a while to decide what advice this conjured mom of mine would give.

Maybe: "When you break up, you lose the person you tell things to—the person you talk to about your day, about a funny moment, or what makes you mad. It takes time to replace that."

Then she'd pass me a spoon of something to try. Something good. Something better than peanut butter on stale bread.

It sounds stupid to say I miss my mom, like I'm some kid left at kindergarten for the first time. I'm almost ready to graduate and move out and then I wouldn't see her anyway, so what's the big difference? And what does she know about losing people? My dad and I are the ones who had to learn about that.

My eyes are watering, probably because of the imaginary onions.

When the phone rings, it's Greg, saying that everyone's going to Dallas's house. I figure I'd better grab the lifeline before I make up any more conversations and lose my mind altogether.

He says to pick him up at nine. I glance at the driveway to make sure Dad left the truck, and then I agree. It looks like I'm the designated driver for the evening, which I'm not thrilled about. House parties in Webster tend to be the same fifty kids you saw after school, except milling around someone's kitchen instead of standing at their lockers. It takes a beer or two to make it seem more interesting than that.

Pick up Greg at nine o'clock. There are still five hours to fill.

Bored, roaming through the silent house, I find myself in our wood-paneled downstairs rec room. I'm standing in front of the east wall, which is lined floor to ceiling and corner to corner with bookshelves. Mom was an English major. She was going to be a professor until she met Dad and became a high school teacher instead. If she were still around, she would have been my lit teacher next year. Having my mom lecture me about books would have been nothing new.

"TV rots your brain," she used to nag, taking away the remote control and plunking a book in my hand.

I wonder how she'd feel now that my movies and my film books have taken over a few of her shelves. Randomly, I pull out the *Project Grizzly* disc and pop it into the machine.

Project Grizzly.

It's the first documentary I can remember watching. When I was seven, or maybe eight, I walked into the living room and found Dad focused on the screen. There was a man on TV dressed in the strangest armor I'd ever laid eyes on.

"Come over here. Have a look at this idiot," Dad said.

So I sat cross-legged on the carpet below his chair and we watched as the armored man got smacked with a flying log. He was trying to create a bear-proof suit that would allow him to safely stalk a grizzly. It looked like an astronaut costume, and he could barely walk in it. He couldn't even get in or out of it without his friends' help.

"What kind of idiot . . . ?" my dad kept saying, but with a little admiration in his voice.

Even my mom got drawn in after a while, and all three of us sat there shaking our heads in unison.

In the years since that first viewing, I've learned that the National Film Board made *Project Grizzly*. Apparently, it's a personal favorite of Quentin Tarantino—which proves how twisted it is.

I turn it off, finally, when my stomach starts growling. As the microwave spins my pizza, I'm still thinking about the bear-obsessed man and all the guys helping him out. Did they really have nothing better to do than watch their friend try to kill himself?

I do my dishes. In case the spirit of my mom's still lingering around, cutting onions, I even wipe the counters. That's when I spot the brochure Ms. Gladwell gave me. It has somehow migrated to the stack of papers beside the microwave.

VANCOUVER FILM STUDIO
A PREMIER ENTERTAINMENT ARTS INSTITUTION

The cover is black matte with a makeup artist's rendition of a monster along one side.

It stares at me. I flip it over.

Do you have a vision? A need to tell stories? A distinctive way of looking at the world? Your time at the studio will help you explore your talents with an eye to becoming an industry-ready filmmaker. It's time to realize your unique creative voice.

Unique creative voice. I could have one of those. Maybe.

I've heard of the studio before, of course. Quite a few famous directors and actors have studied there. I've even glanced at the school's website before. But now I get a churning feeling in my gut when I think about the place. Because it could be real. One year from today, I could be blowing town and heading to Vancouver.

It's the year of change, right?

Maybe I should call it the year of escape.

I grab a handful of cookies from the cupboard and head downstairs to the computer. The studio's home page features the same image as the brochure. I click on the tab for admissions information.

Step 1: Application. Forms available for download. Deadline for early admission is January 15.

Step 2: Financial Aid. I won't need a loan, mainly because of Mom's life-insurance settlement. Thanks, Mom.

Step 3: Portfolio.

What the heck's a portfolio? When I click on that third

item, a list of options drops down. Then cookie crumbs spray from my mouth onto the keyboard.

The phone rings—Greg again. He's ready early.

"What kind of high school student has a portfolio?" I mutter, half to Greg and half to myself.

"A what?" Greg says.

"For film school. It says I have to send a portfolio."

"A what?"

"Exactly." I skim through the suggested materials. "It says I can send clips of myself onstage . . . acting in or directing a school play . . . my makeup work . . . a short . . ."

"Stop there," Greg says. "I'd go for the short one."

"They mean a short film."

"Well, you could do that," he says, as if the matter's settled. "You're always filming crap anyway."

"Not anything interesting."

"Come pick me up, and we'll brainstorm."

Sure, we'll brainstorm. But unless Greg can storm up some way to make my life a million times more interesting or arrange to have a major event occur in my vicinity—preferably while I happen to be holding my camera—I'm in trouble.

The whole season of change is in trouble.

chapter 5

why family members should not appear in public

On the way to Dallas's house, I scan the side streets and store-fronts as if ideas might leap out at me. I already know that if I make a short, it'll be a doc. I love all movies, but I've always pictured myself making films about real events. Something set in a war zone with bullets flying as I piece together the truth of what's happening, broadcasting it to the world. Or maybe a hard-hitting investigation of corporate corruption.

It's possible I've seen too many Peter Snow and Michael Moore interviews.

Webster has a distinct lack of war zones and corporate offices, and Greg's not helping me concentrate. Whooping and hollering tunelessly to the blaring stereo, he begs me to spin a doughnut in the grocery store parking lot just so we can cruise Canyon Street one more time before going to the party. As if you can spin in a four-wheel-drive pickup. As if we might discover something new. I'm quickly coming to the conclusion that film topics are as likely to appear as werewolves or vampires.

"Let's just go to Dallas's place," I yell over the bass.

Dallas's name isn't really Dallas, it's Mark. But there were already a dozen Marks in school when he moved here a couple years ago, and his Texas accent was such a novelty, he got pegged with "Dallas" before he had a choice.

The parties are always at his house these days, hosted by either him or his older brother or both. His mom's still in Texas for some reason, and his dad works out of town half the time. Plus, the house is such a wreck that a party or two doesn't seem to make a difference.

Tonight, when Greg and I walk in, the crowd in the kitchen falls suddenly silent and Greg's beer opens with a pop that seems loud and obscene. Everyone's staring at me.

Then the volume rises again.

"Hear you're back on the prowl," a guy says, going for a high five.

So that's it. They've heard about the breakup. I'm surprised it took this long. Maybe Lauren thought she could keep it quiet, we'd get back together, and no one would know the difference.

There are a few more elbows and wisecracks from the guys in the kitchen. Two girls in the corner roll their eyes and slide from the room. Eventually, I make it through the gauntlet and flop onto Dallas's sagging tweed couch. I've barely flipped open my video camera—for the sake of practice—when a waft of something like cinnamon and flowers floats over me. A curtain of hair swings into the viewfinder, followed by the rest of Hannah Deprez.

If Hannah's not the brightest star in the sky, she makes up for it in pure hotness. Greg says one day she'll end up like her mother, who he describes as a mini-marshmallow in a lot of makeup. Doesn't matter. At this moment in time, Hannah's gorgeous. She's got long, dark hair and big brown eyes and quite possibly the most attractive lips I've ever seen. They're pouting at my camera.

I turn it off.

"I thought you were never going to show up, Cole," she says. Did I mention Hannah's voice? She could have a part-time job performing phone sex. I'm not exaggerating.

"I heard you and Lauren broke up." She wiggles into a spot between me and the arm of the couch.

"Yeah. We . . . uh . . ."

"You doing okay?" She has her fingers in my hair.

I nod.

She must be drunk because the next thing I know, she's kissing me. Not that I object. Hannah's lips are . . . dexterous. She nibbles my top lip and pulls at my bottom lip and in between skirts her tongue along the edges of my mouth. She has one hand on my jaw, her thumb on my cheek, and tendrils of hair brushing my neck. My own hand is climbing a path from the back of her waistband underneath her shirt to her bra strap.

When she pulls my hand away, I think the fun's over for the evening. But it's just because she's seen the door to Dallas's dad's bedroom open. She tugs me inside and soon we're lying on the bed together creating our own version of *Porndemic*.

"Hang on a sec," Hannah says, pulling away. She puts one of her iPod earphones in my ear. "So we can listen to the same song," she whispers, snuggling against me.

Girl music. And Hannah's head is on my shoulder as if I've found myself a new girlfriend in thirty minutes flat.

"I've wanted to play this for you ever since I heard about your mom," she says. "I didn't feel like I knew you well enough. The song's all about loss. And hope . . ."

Suddenly, I find my mojo draining away. Why am I in a bedroom listening to chick music? I mean, making out with Hannah was all right—quite good, actually—but it seems to have ended now and an unwelcome heaviness settles over me. This happens sometimes. And I hate it. I hate that I'm in bed with the sexiest girl in school and I'm staring at a stain on the ceiling instead of at her cleavage.

The stain looks like a chicken.

"You know, I made a roast chicken a while ago. With potatoes and everything."

"Really? Cool." She's scrolling through her playlist, trying to find another song she wants me to hear. Maybe she thinks this one's about us.

"Yeah. It was good. Then Mr. Gill said something in class a few days later about not sliding backward. I think he meant that we shouldn't forget to study, but to me it meant . . . what am I trying to prove?"

"Yeah." She nods.

"I mean, what difference is a roast chicken going to make?"

"A roast chicken?"

"Exactly. Not going to change the world. Not going to change my life or my dad's life. It's not going to do anything. It's like pretending my mom's still around. From this point forward, there will be no re-creating the past. It's going to be all about trying new things."

"I'm new," Hannah says. She is, relatively. Her family moved to Webster last year, and her arrival caused a shift in the tectonic plates of the school social system. When the same girls have been in your class since kindergarten, the introduction of a new one is somewhat . . . seismic.

"You *are* new," I agree, ignoring the way she's started kissing my neck again. "Although, I don't need everything to be new. It's more that I need to distance myself. I'm surrounded by all these people who want things from me or need me to be around. They're like a dog pack."

"The pack mentality," Hannah murmurs. I'm surprised she's actually listening. "Mentality" seems like a big word for her. She taps a finger against her lips, as if considering my point. When she catches me watching, she moves her hand to her hair, riffling it over her shoulder.

"Sort of," I say. "What I need is to detach, free myself to leave town next year. But apparently I have to create a film before I can do that . . ."

Hannah is taking her bra off.

"You know what I think?" she says. "Too much talking."

Is it? I'm not sure I'm fit for anything else.

Then Hannah's breasts distract me from the chicken stain. She has my undivided attention until someone pounds on the door.

Dallas pokes his big Texan nose inside, complaining about not being able to find a bed at his own party. Hannah makes a grab for her shirt, and a few minutes later, we emerge into the crush of people. She leans against me. I'm not entirely sure if she's nuzzling my neck or if she's just having trouble staying upright.

That's when I hear, above Hannah's murmurs, a gasp that

makes my blood rush out of my crotch and back to my brain. Lauren is standing at the door to the living room.

Shit. I haven't disengaged Hannah's lips yet, but she must realize I've turned into some sort of ice sculpture beside her. She pulls away, looks at my face, and then follows my gaze. We both stare at Lauren as if we've been caught at a crime scene.

"Shit." I say it aloud this time, pulling myself from Hannah and tucking in my shirt as I crisscross the room to get to Lauren. She's turned to leave already—but not before I saw the look on her face.

I catch up to her on the back porch. She's standing with her arms wrapped tightly around herself.

"Sorry." It seems like the best way to start.

"Yeah, you really looked sorry," she says. Her voice is cold, but I know her well enough to see she's trying not to cry. I *am* actually sorry, though more sorry that she saw Hannah and me together than sorry that we were together. I'm guessing that Lauren won't appreciate the subtle distinction if I try to explain.

"Hannah's drunk. She started coming on to me. . . ."

"Sure, Cole. You had nothing to do with it. Right."

"Hey, I didn't mean to hurt your feelings. But we're broken up." I said I was sorry, right? "We were kissing. That's it. It didn't mean anything."

Lauren wheels on me. "Maybe it didn't to you," she says

sharply, jabbing her finger at my chest. "Because apparently you feel no emotion. To those of us who have feelings, those of us who thought that you and I meant something, that we were going somewhere, that we were going to be something together—then it's a little earth shattering."

I run a hand through my hair. What I'd really like to do is jump over the porch railing and make a run for my truck.

"I'm sorry. Really."

She glares.

"What else do you want me to say?"

"Figure it out." Sarcasm drips from her words the way juice drips from a just-bitten pear. Then Lauren bashes past me in a move that's bound to leave a bruise on her shoulder, and she's gone. When I return to the kitchen a few minutes later, she's nowhere in sight. Probably crying to her friend Lex somewhere.

I stand there for a minute, feeling the heaviness pour back with a load of guilt on top. How exactly did my night go so wrong? A few minutes ago I was making out with a gorgeous girl, no strings attached. I should have climbed out the window of the bedroom afterward and avoided all this mess.

I weave my way back through the party, nodding when someone yells something that I can't hear over the music and shaking my head when Dallas waves a beer in my direction.

Hannah's disappeared. I find Greg flipping bottle caps at a guy wearing only boxer shorts. Lost a bet, apparently.

"I've got to head out," I yell in Greg's ear. "You coming or staying?"

"Coming!" He snaps one more cap and hits the guy on the inner thigh. Grinning at the yelp he causes, Greg turns and barrels a path for us.

After the noise of the party, the cab of the truck seems perfectly, absolutely still. I sigh and lean against the steering wheel before I turn the key. The sky's clear, so clear the Milky Way shows up as a ghostly cloudlike wisp behind the stars.

Greg must be looking at it too. He says, "If I told you I'd seen little green men, would you believe me?"

"How much have you had to drink?"

"I'm not saying I *have* seen little green men. I'm just asking . . . if I told you I'd seen them, would you believe me?"

I pull my camera out of my pocket. This conversation begs to be recorded.

"If you were serious, completely serious, then I'd believe that *you* believed that you'd seen aliens," I say.

"See, that's the problem, right there. You'd believe that I believed I'd seen them. That's not good enough."

"It's not?"

"No. The group therapist at whatever asylum my parents sent me to would probably say that exact same thing. I'm thinking there has to be someone in the world who will believe me no matter what."

I've had these conversations with Greg before. For a future mechanic, the guy can wax philosophical when he feels the urge. I reach over and slap a hand on his shoulder. "Bud, I'd believe you," I promise.

"For sure?"

"Absolutely."

We sit in silence for another minute until the door to Dallas's house opens and slams shut and a group of hollering yahoos heads in our direction. I start the engine and peel out.

"You think men on other planets have woman issues to deal with?" I ask as we head down the road.

Greg nods sagely. "Definitely. No escaping them, man. They don't get better, either. You should hear my mom and dad these days. It's nuclear meltdown waiting to happen."

"Seriously?"

"Seriously. Radioactive."

We drive back toward town with the windows rolled down and the stereo up, the bass trying to beat the confusion from my skull. By the time we're rolling down Canyon Street, I'm feeling more relaxed. So relaxed, that I almost don't notice the man walking—weaving—down the sidewalk with the curvy blonde.

"Isn't that . . . ?" Greg bolts upright in the passenger seat and cranes his neck as we pass.

"What?"

"That was your dad! With a woman." By the way he says "woman," I can tell it's not the first word he was going to choose.

"If this is a test to see whether I'll believe you at all times, I won't."

"This is not a test. That was your dad."

"Weird."

"Aren't you going to turn around? I think he was waving at you."

Turning around is exactly the last thing I want to do. I have this feeling in the pit of my stomach that says if I turn around, I'm going to regret it. I may as well push the pedal to the floor, crash into the wall of Burger Barn, and hope for a better outcome.

I slow down and glance in the rearview mirror. A bad decision. They're a block behind us now, but Dad's definitely waving me down.

Swearing, I swing into the Burger Barn parking lot.

"Watch it!" Greg yells. "You just about hit the wall."

"Yeah, yeah. Just about."

After all my talk of detaching myself, my dad waves, and I immediately stop to see what he needs. I obviously suck at this. I need some of Greg's little green aliens to pop down and abduct me. They can drop me in a forest somewhere and I won't ever have to meet this blonde.

chapter 6

do not go gently

I make a U-turn and drive back to my dad, pulling over to the side of the road. Greg rolls down his window and Dad swings his elbow up to rest on the edge. He misses, staggers, and tries again, managing to prop himself. The woman stays on the sidewalk, giggling a little.

"What'd I tell ya?" Dad says to her. "I knew he seen us. He's a good kid."

In a film, this shot would be a wide angle from down the street. Then the camera would slowly dolly toward us, the geometric lines of the sidewalk giving way to the shine of the streetlight on the truck hood and the shimmer of this woman in sequins.

Dad's "friend" is wearing a shiny black skirt that barely hides her crotch. A tiny tank top's stretched over a rather un-tiny body. My eyes plunge into her cleavage before I can tear them away. Which is gross. She's maybe not as old as my dad, but she's way too old to be showing that much cleavage. She has breast wrinkles. The camera would capture those.

Dad turns to me. "Whatcha say you give your old man and his friend a ride home?"

I can't answer him because I'm not sure exactly what will happen if I unclench my jaw. Either I'm going to throw up or I'm going to swear at him. What is he doing staggering down Canyon Street with this woman? What if there's a heaven up there and Mom is seeing all this? She'd probably die a second death.

First Lauren goes nuts and now this. I should have stayed home tonight.

Greg is looking back and forth between my dad and me as if he's a spectator at a tennis match. Suddenly, he grabs his baseball cap off the console. "I'm going to hike up the hill from here. Thanks for the ride, Cole. See ya, Mr. Owens." Innocent dumb-boy-mechanic act.

"Get in," I growl at my dad, still trying to talk without moving my teeth.

For them both to fit into the cab of the truck, my dad has to hike one butt cheek onto the center console, leaving the blonde woman enough room to sit if she plants half of her fat ass on Dad's lap. Which she does willingly. I try to stare straight ahead so I don't vomit.

"I'm Sheri," she says, extending a hand over Dad and toward me. I keep both hands clutching the wheel, my knuckles white.

"Oh, I suppose I shoulda officially introduced you." Dad gives a fake guffaw, spewing beer breath at me. You'd think that after Dallas's party, I'd be immune to the smell, but apparently not.

"Where to, Sheri?" I ask.

Of course she lives down across the highway, back near Dallas's house, which means we have to drive like this for five excruciating minutes, Sheri whispering and giggling in Dad's ear, Dad laughing at her jokes as if she were a stand-up comedian, and me pretending I'm somewhere else. Like Antarctica.

"You have a nice night now," Sheri coos when she finally slides herself out the door. "Good to meet you, Cole."

The prospect of having to drive home with Dad talking about Sheri is worse than actually driving with Sheri.

"Have a good time?" I ask sarcastically.

"Guess I got a little carried away," he says.

Maybe he doesn't want to talk about it either because he flops his head back and closes his eyes as soon as we pull out of Sheri's driveway. And by the time we're halfway home, he's snoring. I have to help him into the house when we get there. I dump him on his bed and take off his shoes, but that's it. There's no way I'm undressing him. If he hurls on the carpet, he can clean it up himself.

"Everything go okay last night, bud?" Greg asks as we slide into the booth at Burger Barn.

I'm filming the scene around us, ketchup smears and all. If I'd had my camera ready during last night's scene with Lauren, I would have had the perfect start to a documentary about messy breakups. So I've decided to film everything—even things as universally uninteresting as Burger Barn—until drama erupts again.

"I dropped her off," I say, turning the lens on Greg. "Then I hauled my dad into bed. He probably won't even remember. He was still sleeping when I left."

Maybe no one else will remember either. Maybe Dad and the bar wench managed to stagger downtown without a single person driving by. Maybe no one noticed me and Hannah at the party last night, and maybe no one will ask what's going on between us. Maybe she won't call me today wanting to "hang out" as if we're suddenly boyfriend and girlfriend. Maybe no one heard Lauren and me arguing on the back porch and no one cared. And maybe hell will freeze over, pigs will fly, and Webster will turn out *not* to be a pit of incestuous gossip.

Lauren used to tell me that gossip was a sign of a tight community. She said women talk about people so they know each other's needs.

I'm pretty sure that's messed up.

"Could you turn the camera off? Why are you looking at me like that?" Greg asks as he dips a handful of fries in ketchup and stuffs them in his mouth. I realize I'm scowling.

"Sorry. I was just thinking that this place sucks."

"Yeah, the food stinks." He finishes the last of his fries. "Hey, I gotta go to Sanford today. My dad needs a part for the shop, and my mom's driving me crazy. She threatened to ground me for leaving the milk on the counter."

"Ground you?"

"I know. Like I'm eight. Anyway, I'm getting out of here. You wanna come?"

Sanford. That's exactly what I need. I mean, Sanford's only an hour away and it's a piss hole of a city, if it can even be called a city, but it's somewhere other than here.

Half an hour later, we're ripping up the highway with the windows open and the stereo pounding. As we pass the last fruit stand, evergreens replace the orchards along the side of the road. I start thinking about Greg's messed-up family again. His mom is a little . . . odd. As in *Welcome to the Dollhouse* odd.

"Remember how your mom used to give us those home-made fruit leathers?"

Greg shudders. "Like purple tarpaper."

She made us other snacks too, back when we used to hang out in the yard, climbing the willow tree to get away from Greg's little sister. We were fed cookies made with applesauce instead of sugar. Green smoothies. Pizza pockets with whole-wheat dough and vegetarian soybean filling. We called those "poison pockets." Greg's mom is the dietician at a seniors' home, which probably affects the town's death rate.

I feel a stab of guilt. It's kind of against the rules to disrespect someone else's mom. Besides, I have enough problems with my own family, what's left of it. Dad's going to wake up to an empty house and I didn't leave a message or a note behind. There's no cell service on the highway. I didn't even stop at home after our burgers. I just wanted out of town.

"This is stupid," I mutter.

"What?" Greg yells over the music.

"I'm feeling guilty about leaving my dad on his own. It's stupid! He's an adult."

"Yeah, man. And he was out of it last night. He'll probably sleep for the whole day. What've you got to feel guilty about?"

"Good question."

But I do. With just the two of us now, it feels as if I'm part of a mandatory group project, like in health class. Create a mural-size collage about body image or something equally stupid. Normally, you'd skip the whole assignment. Who cares about grades in health class? But every minute of work you miss is a minute that your partner is handling without you, and soon the guilt is so crippling that you're cutting and gluing as if body image issues are your own personal passion.

I scratch a hand through my hair. I don't need to be thinking about mandatory teamwork right now.

"You're right. Dad can take care of himself today."

"True."

"And he has friends, right?"

"Last night he sure did." Greg smirks.

"Shut up. My point is, he doesn't need me hanging out with him every second of the weekend."

"Exactly."

Minutes later, Greg's singing—badly—to the stereo. I join in, letting the noise of it fill me, blank out the space between my ears. Dangling an arm out the window, I can almost catch the wind. It feels good. Temptingly good.

Unsnapping my seat belt, I reach outside to grab the roof of the car and pull myself out until I'm sitting on the window's edge, the wind whipping my hair, making my eyes water, and tearing every unwanted thought from my head.

Greg hollers in approbation. Nothing but trees and patches of marsh line the road. Filling my lungs with the rushing air, I yell. Not words, just sound. And it feels like a total release. If this were a movie, we would keep driving until we flew over the edge of the world.

As the song ends and another begins, Greg's head pops out of the other window.

"What are you doing?" I yell. But I'm laughing.

"I can steer with my toes!" he screams.

We're on a long straight stretch, so he can steer, but he can't hold down the gas pedal. It doesn't take long before we're coasting more and more slowly down the road. We ripple our way back through the windows and into our seats as a semi truck rounds the corner just ahead.

"Too late!" I yell. "Show's over!"

We snap our seat belts back in place, glowing with our own ridiculousness. The semi blows by us, rocking our car in its backwash. Greg hits the gas. Leaning my head back, I close my eyes, letting the bass vibrate my sternum.

The brakes screech loud and long.

I'm thrown hard against the seat belt, my arms flinging forward like scarecrow limbs, out of my control. Swearing, Greg wrenches the wheel. Our back end slides, but not fast enough. There's a deer frozen in front of us, a tableau painting in frail browns, wide eyes. There's a crunch—a snap?—and all I can see in the windshield is speckled fur, a close-up of surprising detail. I swear I see each hair, etched in relief. Then it's gone as the animal slides back down the hood. There's another crunch, the splinter of cracking glass, and silence. The car rocks to a stop.

"Shit." Greg is the first to speak.

I check to see if I'm breathing and make sure I haven't pissed my own pants. The radio is still blaring. I flick the music off.

"You okay?"

Greg nods. The inside of the car looks exactly the same, but the windshield is a spiderweb of cracks.

Slowly, reluctantly, we both open our doors and climb out. The deer is lying on the road in front of the car and even from where I'm standing, I can see its side heaving. It's alive.

Greg and I walk toward it, peer at it. It's sprawled out the way dogs sometimes laze on hot asphalt, soaking in sun, though one of its legs is bent at an unnatural angle. There's no blood. The creature tries to stand and fails. It can't lift more than its head. It stares up at us with huge, panic-filled eyes.

"We're scaring it," I say.

We both step backward.

"I don't think it's going to live," Greg says.

"No way it's going to live. We hit it like a freight train."

Greg takes another step away, as if the deer might hear us. "Do you think it knows it's dying?" he asks. "I mean . . . do you think animals can understand that, or do you think it just knows it's in pain?"

"I think maybe just the pain." I have no freaking idea.

"I don't have anything to kill it with," Greg says.

I guess I've been existing in the present tense, like the deer, because it hasn't occurred to me that we're going to have to kill it. My stomach turns at the thought. I've never been one to load up the gun rack and head into the woods. There's a lot of that around Webster, but I always figured the meat at the grocery store was fresh enough for me.

"We could whack it with something," I say finally. Simultaneously, we look to the trees, but they're on the other side of the ditch and the thought of marching across, finding a branch big enough to knock out a deer, and then actually hitting the creature—that's enough to hold us both in place.

We're standing there stupidly, arms crossed over our chests, when a pickup truck comes down the road. The driver pulls over and flicks on his hazard lights. Something we should have done, I suppose.

It's an older guy, my dad's age.

"You boys all right?" he asks. We both nod.

"The deer's not looking so good," Greg says.

"I can see that." He turns back to his truck. For a brief moment, I think he's leaving, and I fight the urge to throw myself at his ankles and beg him not to go. Stupid. We're not in danger. We're fine. We can handle a half-dead deer.

The man comes back with a rifle from behind his seat.

"Either of you boys want to do this?"

We both shake our heads.

We don't turn away when he shoots, though. It wouldn't be right. We stand and watch him raise the barrel, aim carefully, shoot with a blast that echoes against the trees and the mountains behind them. There's a small spurt of blood from the deer's head and I'm sure, absolutely sure, that I will be able to re-create that miniature red fountain in my mind for the rest of my life.

The deer's chest stops heaving. I stare at the mottled fur on its side to make sure.

"We'll just pull it to the shoulder and the highways department will pick it up," the man says.

So we grab a leg each, in what seems like a sordid act, and we pull the deer onto the gravel. It's surprisingly heavy for something that looks so delicate.

"You need a ride?" the man asks.

Greg shakes his head. "The car should still get us home. Thanks for your help."

As the guy drives away, it strikes me: I asked for a disaster and one occurred. And I didn't record any of it.

"Damn. I should have been filming."

"Seriously?" Greg says.

I shrug. "I have to make a short to get into film school, remember?"

"About roadkill?"

"Hang on, I'm going to grab my camera."

I admit, it feels wrong. It feels wrong to zoom in on a dead deer.

Instead of worrying about the ethics of the situation, I try to think like a filmmaker. Objectively. With distance. Maybe, by filming the deer, I'm fulfilling a sort of responsibility. I'm documenting the event, ensuring that its death will affect people, mean something.

But the objectivity/emotional distance plan doesn't work. Already, I can tell that when I close my eyes tonight, I'm going to replay this creature's death as if my eyelids were a theater screen.

I snap the camera shut. The whole idea was crazy, I suppose.

Greg certainly thinks so. He doesn't say it. He just shakes his head, waits for me to climb into the car, and then makes a U-turn, pointing the crumpled hood back toward town.

"What if that had happened when we were leaning out the windows?" he says after a while.

I don't answer.

He glances at me. "Do you think that deer was supposed to die at that exact moment, or do you think we could have avoided it?"

I had this exact conversation with Lauren, months ago. She thinks death happens randomly, but God creates something good from it. Which I think is a load of crap, and I told her so. Whether or not my mom was destined to die, it sucked. And nothing was going to make that better, not even God.

"What am I, an expert on death?" I ask Greg. "How the hell am I supposed to know?"

"Sorry," he says after a minute.

But I *am* the expert. I know all sorts of things that Greg and Lauren have no way of understanding. I know that death sneaks up on you when you're not paying attention. It doesn't help to expect it or try to escape it. You can only insulate yourself so it hurts less when you get hit.

Greg tilts his head back and forth, trying to find an angle that allows him to actually see through the glass.

I find myself blinking fast and I turn away slightly, staring at the oozing body of a bug that's squished at the end of the windshield's longest crack.

"I don't think roadkill's a good choice for your film," Greg says finally.

"No," I agree.

I don't want to make a film about roadkill.

chapter 7

what happens when mouth and brain disconnect

After explaining the smashed windshield to Greg's dad, I bump into Hannah and head to Dallas's house for a much needed drink. It's well after midnight when I start walking along Canyon Street toward home.

In front of Burger Barn, where I picked up Dad the other night, I stop.

Not because I'm thinking about Dad and Sheri—I am resolutely *not* thinking about Dad and Sheri—but because the image of Greg's windshield has given me an idea for my film. The way the cracks spread out from the point of impact, the whole thing looked about to shatter. And yet, somehow, the shards were still attached to one another. That image, with some atmospheric adhering to it. For example, when I was hauling Dad to bed last night and noticed that his fly was undone, I stayed quiet. Did I want to race to the bathroom and puke? Yes. Did I want to grab Dad by the neck and ask why he was whoring around with Mom's memory? Maybe. The point is, I didn't.

Now Dad's sitting in my space and asking questions.

"Have a good time tonight?"

"Not bad," I say.

Silence. I wonder if he even knows that I broke up with Lauren. Should I tell him? I hesitate. I can't figure out how to start. And I don't really want to discuss relationships.

"What are you doing down here?" I say finally.

"Can't a man sit in his own house?"

I'm not convinced. Probably because he's sitting in Mom's chair with an unopened book in his lap—*Pride and Prejudice*, of all things—and he's never read a Victorian novel in his life. I'm pretty sure he's never sat in that chair in his life.

"Why aren't you upstairs watching TV?"

"Came down to check on you."

"I'm good."

I peer at him closely. It looks as if his eyes are red. Maybe he's been drinking. Or taking Viagra. It occurs to me that Dad and are not exactly close. Mom used to span the gap between us.

"How about you?" I ask. "Did you go out?"

lighting; flashed among images of spiderwebs, maybe, or nets; and spliced with interviews of people who live in Webster, each wrapped in a personal, complicated web . . .

I'm still sorting through ideas as I unlock the basement door to find Dad sitting downstairs waiting for me. He's in the armchair by Mom's bookshelves, the reading lamp casting a circle of light like an island around the chair. I stop well offshore.

"Little late, isn't it, Cole?" he grumbles.

My first thought is that Greg's dad has called him about the accident. But he doesn't look concerned or mad. He's just sitting there.

"Are you waiting up for me?"

I resist the urge to wipe any of Hannah's remaining lipstick off my neck.

Before Mom died, we functioned on "trust" principles. I supposed to call if I ended up doing something different what I had told her I would be doing. For example, if said I was going to dinner with Greg but we ended ing Monopoly with Lauren's family (her family actu Monopoly), I was supposed to call. It was a good syste just enough that we could both pretend she always I was.

Dad, on the other hand, has always operate ask-don't-tell system, and we've been pretty

"Not tonight."

"So."

"Yeah."

There's another silence. It's probably short in reality, but it seems to stretch like the Golden Gate Bridge, strung with lights and potential suicide jumpers.

This is what should happen at this point: Dad should grunt, heave himself out of the chair, and head upstairs.

I might say something like: "Dad? Is there something you wanted to talk about?"

He'd say, "Nah."

"Okay," I'd reply. I wouldn't believe him, but I'd be relieved. In a way, it's good that we're not too close. In another year, we'll be splitting up. Moving on with separate lives.

"It's late, Cole. Go to bed," he'd finish.

"Same to you."

That's not what happens.

"You're not keeping Sheri company tonight?" The question pops out of my mouth. I want to bite off my tongue as soon as I hear the words. I thought I'd just decided we *wouldn't* discuss relationships. What do I care about Sheri? And if Dad's not thinking about her right now, why am I reminding him?

"She's working."

"Now?" I need to stop asking about her. But it's the middle

of the night, and who works in the middle of the night? Sheri didn't have that "nurse on night shift" look to me. And she definitely wasn't the doctor on call.

"She works late," Dad says.

And then I know. I understand what should have been obvious the first time I met Sheri. She's a—

No. I'm not going to ask. I don't want to hear the answer. This conversation should be over, right here.

"What exactly does Sheri do?" There I go again. The words come flying out of my mouth without my permission. My mind doesn't seem connected to my tongue tonight. Maybe I have one of those brain injuries that knocks out your ability to edit your thoughts. Or Tourette's syndrome. That's probably it. I have sudden-onset Tourette's.

"She's a dancer," Dad says as he pushes himself out of the reading chair the way he was supposed to five minutes ago. He heads upstairs without meeting my stare.

"That's great." Just great. She's a stripper.

Once he's gone, I realize I didn't even tell him about the deer. I turn off the lamp, flop into Mom's chair, and see again the spurt of blood from the animal's skull. How many spurts before something's really and truly dead? Does the brain know it's dead before the heart or vice versa?

Maybe neither realizes. Maybe there's just darkness. And maybe it's better to go like that. At least it only took a few minutes for the deer.

My mom died of pancreatic cancer. There were only a few months between the diagnosis and her death, months filled with doctors and hospital rooms and words like "malignancy," "adenocarcinoma," and "Trousseau sign," whatever that is.

When someone who's close to you dies, you learn there are a lot of things people don't talk about. I mean, there's that whole Hollywood scene where you sit by the side of the hospital bed breathing in urine and antiseptic and you share memories, as if they'll hold you safely in the past. "Hey, Mom, remember the time you taught me how to run the Slinky down the stairs? That was cool."

That really happens, just like in the movies.

There are other things that don't get said aloud. We never said "you're dying" or "terminal cancer" or "when you're dead." Soon the doctors were saying "palliative," and I knew that *meant* "dying," but I still never said it, and neither did Mom. Maybe Mom and Dad said it when they were together and I wasn't there. I doubt it. Why say what you already know?

Afterward, when she was gone, there was a whole bunch of new ways for everyone to avoid talking about what actually happened. At school, teachers said, "I'm sorry for your loss." The gym teacher put his hand on my shoulder and said, "Heard you've had a rough time of it." No one ever, ever said, "Sorry your mom's dead." Which was okay, I suppose. It just left this big circle of silence inside me, like the blackened ring of stones around an old bonfire pit.

On the day of the funeral, there was a wake at our house.

I'm not sure how that day got planned, to tell you the truth. Dad and I were shuttled from our front door to the funeral parlor, then the cemetery, then back into our driveway. When we reentered our house, chairs had been pushed along the edges of all the walls and the kitchen table was loaded with sandwiches, grocery-store fruit-and-cheese platters, plastic jugs of pop, and stacks of plates and napkins and cups.

Greg and Dallas were in the living room, stuffing their faces with chicken salad rolls. Lauren was there too, flanked by her parents. They stood firm and straight on either side of her like fence posts.

"We're so sorry for your loss," Lauren's mom said.

"Our prayers are with you and your family," her dad said.

Lauren flung herself at me, her arms wrapping around my neck and her whole body pressing against mine. It helped. For a minute, it was like being bandaged.

Then Lauren's mom tapped her shoulder, eyes flashing

"inappropriate display of affection," and Lauren pulled herself away. Her dad passed her a tissue and she dabbed beneath her lashes.

So formal.

If Lauren and I were together for twenty more years, would we sit at family gatherings like TV news anchors with lacquered faces and insincere smiles? I wanted to ask her parents. And I wanted to ask why they were already drawing Lauren toward the door. Did they think cancer was contagious? Or death?

Then someone else put a hand on my shoulder and had more meaningless words to share, and I never did get to ask my questions. Which was better, I suppose. Inappropriate display of aggression.

"You should eat something, sweetheart," one of Mom's friends told me, and put a plate of sandwiches in my hands. I was happy to eat. Starving, actually. But it didn't seem right to stand in the middle of those people—did they all actually know my mother?—and scarf sandwiches. I took myself across the landing and sat in the semidark at the top of the basement stairs, listening to the murmur of hushed conversations.

I had polished off one tuna fish and two egg salad halves and I was just starting on the ham and cheese when I heard my name. You know how voices can surround you, all running into one another like the colors in an oily puddle, and then someone says your name and it's like a car tire driving through the puddle? That's what happened.

"Cole must be devastated."

"I can't get over how fast it happened." That was Aunt Claire, my dad's sister from Saskatoon. There was a crack in her voice that made my throat want to close. I had to stop chewing until I'd taken a few deep breaths.

"Such a tragedy." That was Mom's best friend, Lily Daniels. She and her husband own an orchard on the east side of town. When I was small, I used to climb all the trees, one after another, while Mom and Mrs. Daniels had coffee.

"At least he's practically grown up," my aunt said, sounding like she was trying to pull herself together.

"Poor Douglas, though. He'll be on his own," Mrs. Daniels said.

Cue background music. Something tragic and orchestral.

Why would she say something like that? We were grown men. We could manage. We'd already been managing the whole time Mom was in the hospital.

"Damn it," I muttered. Damn the funeral, the wake, Lauren's family, and the entire stuck-eating-on-the-stairs situation.

Aunt Claire and Mrs. Daniels must have heard me because they both scurried away. I couldn't look at them for the rest of the wake. I could barely look at anyone.

● ● ●

Lauren picks up groceries on Monday afternoons. She says her mom finds the store overwhelming—too many people, too many fluorescent lights. So Lauren goes instead. Every Monday.

I know this. So if I happen to be driving past the grocery store at three o'clock on Monday, is that a coincidence or is my subconscious screwing with me?

She's walking along the side of the road with Lex, both of them lugging canvas bags. I pull over and roll down the window.

"Can I give you a ride?"

Lauren's cheeks are flushed and strands of her hair have escaped her ponytail.

"We're fine," Lex says, barely glancing up from the sidewalk.

"You sure? It's baking out there."

Lauren hesitates.

Lex is a few steps ahead when she realizes her friend has stopped. She sighs. "Fine. Go," she says. "You can take my bags. I'll meet you at your house."

"You can squeeze in," I tell Lex.

"Not likely," she says. She's looking at me like I'm a crack dealer or a recently released prison inmate.

"She's feeling a little protective," Lauren says once we've pulled away.

"Between Lex and your mom, it's a miracle we were ever allowed to date in the first place."

She smiles, but only a little. I've broken her golden rule. No one's allowed to speak badly of her family—not even as a joke. She's quiet, straightening her hair, catching the little strands from her neck and retwisting them into her ponytail.

I search for a neutral topic.

"You working this summer?"

"Part time at the library," she says.

"Cool. Maybe you can get them to order some new docs."

"Maybe." She half turns toward me. "Did you actually need to talk to me about something?"

She's not my Lauren anymore. I used to get to see a side of Lauren that no one else knew. A more relaxed Lauren. Someone who could be silly or unexpectedly funny. Now she's smoothed herself into the person that she lets everyone see.

"I just . . . wanted to say hello."

She nods, processing this. "Hello, then," she says.

I wonder how many Laurens there are, really. Are there two—one for public viewing and one for close friends? Or do Lauren's parents and Lex and her other friends each get a different version? Maybe my Lauren was only for me, and now she's gone. That thought stabs me inside, as if I've killed something.

"I'll grab your bags," I say as we pull up at her house.

"Don't bother. I've got them."

Halfway up the walk, she adjusts her grip. Then her shoulders square, and her head tilts up, and her ponytail swings as if it's never had a down day.

I drive away, taking deep breaths.

It felt weird driving with Lauren. But if only our words counted, then maybe it wasn't so bad. On film, you can't show interior monologue. On film, that ride would have seemed normal. Ordinary.

I push away the heavy feeling that's creeping up on me. It's time to move on. I can do this. I can go forward from here.

I'm waiting at the door of the auto shop when Greg gets off work. I like hanging out here. The smell of grease and the sounds of revving engines are the mechanical equivalent of comfort food.

It's not hard to convince Greg to head downtown for dinner after work, but it is hard to get him off the subject of aliens.

"You'd believe me, right? You agreed."

I'm filming him as we walk. If he's going to go bat-shit crazy, at least I'll have a record of his decline.

"If you see aliens, I'll believe you," I assure him. "Because it's important that there's at least one person in the world who will believe you. See? I've been listening."

"But that's not exactly it," he insists.

Now, a big-ass UFO sweeping through the shot at this precise moment—that would be amazing. *That* would be worth filming.

"See, it's one of those paradox things," Greg says. "Unless someone believes me, there's nothing to keep it from happening. A green guy could walk right up to me, punch me in the nose, and there's nothing I could do. I'd be on antipsychotic meds the minute I tried to tell someone."

"So by believing in your aliens, I'm preventing their appearance?"

"Exactly."

Perfect. Bring on the antipsychotic meds for both of us. I turn off the camera. We've reached Canyon Street, and we cross directly in front of the bar.

"You know that woman walking with my dad the other night?" I say.

"Oh, yeah." Greg makes the universal sign for enormous tits.

"Do you think she was a stripper?"

He looks at me sideways. Then he makes the universal sign again.

"Is that a yes?" There's a bad taste at the back of my throat, but I need to confirm this out loud.

"Oh, yeah."

We're at Burger Barn. Cocking an eyebrow at me, Greg

reaches for the NO PARKING sign in front of the door. He wraps a leg around the pole. Then he pumps his hips and pretends to lick the metal.

"Okay, okay, enough." I'm laughing and wincing at the same time. I can't watch.

He starts groaning like a porn soundtrack.

"Boys, do you think that's appropriate behavior for a busy street?" Ms. Gladwell is staring at us. To her credit, she's smiling. Just a bit, though.

Greg stops his gyrations with a cocky smirk, while I wait for the flush of embarrassment to climb my neck and reach my cheeks. Yup. There it is.

As Ms. Gladwell continues down the street, Greg flicks his tongue toward the pole one last time. Then he raises an eyebrow.

"You're completely purple," he says. He turns to look after the counselor. "Hey . . . did you and she really . . ."

"No!"

And my dad didn't screw a stripper. I hope.

chapter 8

the laws of physics and nature, made real

"The Web, take one."

On Tuesday, I drag Greg to the sidewalk in front of the bakery in time to catch the early evening light.

"Here's my concept," I tell him once we're in position. "You live in a small town. It looks peaceful and quaint and perfect. But it's actually a big spiderweb and you're tangled up in the middle of it."

For the right angle—one that includes both Greg and the gingerbread details along the top of the bakery wall—I have to sit on the sidewalk and tilt up the lens. Greg looks as if he has enormous nostrils.

He also looks mildly confused.

"You get the concept, right?"

"I get it," he says.

I press the record button and signal him to begin.

Silence.

"Anytime . . ."

"I haven't figured out what to say."

"Just talk. I'll edit later. Start with something like . . . is Webster as nice as it seems from the outside?"

"It's nice, especially this time of year," he says.

It's hot. That's what Webster is. Hot. The back of my shirt sticks to me, and beads of sweat run down Greg's temples. I stop the camera and make him dab his face. Then we try again.

"I mean from an insider's perspective," I say. "Is Webster really the pretty, peaceful town it looks like on postcards?"

"It's got its problems, I guess. Some of the economy depends on the tourist trade. When tourism's down—"

"What about personally?" I interrupt. "Do you feel trapped here? Isolated from the rest of the world?"

"Sure. Isolated." He's sweating again, and he looks stiff, as if he's standing against a scarecrow pole. His eyes look abnormally round.

This isn't going as well as I'd hoped.

"Just tell me your thoughts on Webster. Whatever comes to mind. And remember, I can edit it afterward."

Ideally, my film would be cinema verité. There would be no formal interviews. Instead, I'd follow my subjects through multiple days and weeks, then edit the vital moments together until the viewer gleaned a sense of their lives.

More realistic to watch, entirely unrealistic to make. It would take me years to create.

"Webster's okay," Greg says. "Not everyone likes small towns. But people here are mostly good, and it's easy to buy land or a house. I mean, I'd like to travel, maybe drive the autobahn. As a place to live, though, Webster's pretty nice."

"What about school? Are you getting out of town for school?"

He looks away. "Still haven't decided."

This is not working. Greg wasn't a good choice for my first interview. He knows it, too. He's looking at me like a kid who's failed a test.

"Cole, can you just tell me what I'm supposed to say?" he asks.

I'd like to. It doesn't seem quite right, though.

I snap the viewfinder closed. "You know what? You were great."

"I sucked," he says.

"I'm sure there's something I can use." It's only the first interview. I have plenty of time to film something that will actually be useful. Repeating this to myself, I manage a reassuring look for Greg.

"Okay." He seems relieved. "Listen, I have to get home. Call me later?"

"Sure. I'll call you."

That's what I'd say if this were an audition. *We'll call you.* Except we wouldn't. Greg would definitely not be on the call-back list.

When I walk into my house, the air is saturated with the sharp, slightly alcoholic tang of gardenia perfume. There's an overstuffed pink purse at the door, flung beside high-heeled white sandals.

"Well, speak of the devil," my dad says from the couch. Judging by the lipstick on his neck, they were *not* just speaking of me. I look from Sheri to him and back again. I'm probably scowling like the devil. My dad is becoming a cliché, right in front of me.

"You're just in time," Sheri chirps, hopping up. "I made paella. It's my absolute spec-ee-ality."

I have no idea what paella is, although it does smell good. Underneath the overwhelming layer of gardenia, that is.

"I think I'll leave you two—" I'll call Greg. No, he was busy. I'll call Hannah. She can pick me up. Getting into a car with Hannah and driving into the dark somewhere sounds about a billion times better than being in this house right now.

"What? A big guy like you, Cole, and you can't eat dinner? C'mon. It's delicious. Did I mention it's my specialty?"

I've heard she has other specialties. I bite my tongue before I say it. My Tourette's syndrome must have been temporary, thank God, because the words stay safely locked inside my head.

Dad is in the kitchen now, dipping a spoon into the electric frying pan, looking as if he's about to swoon. "Stay," he calls, bits of rice spraying from his mouth. "You gotta try this."

"I don't know if you've had paella before," Sheri says, setting me a place at the table. "It's Spanish. A few years ago, I thought, 'Why not try something new?' Turns out I have Spanish in my blood, way back on my mother's side."

If a filmmaker were following *my* life, cinema-verité style, this would be a scene-worthy moment. You really couldn't invent a stranger secondary character than Sheri.

Now that I think about it, the very first feature-length documentary ever made was about the daily life of a family. Granted, it was an Inuit family. I'm pretty sure there wasn't a scene called "Dinner with Dad and the Stripper."

"It's nice to have something a little exotic around here, isn't it, Cole?" Dad beams.

Not particularly, when that something exotic has red lipstick and cleavage like the Grand Canyon. But Dad seems oblivious to the irony. He scoops the paella into a huge casserole dish and sets it in the middle of the table.

I can see sausage slices. And prawns. And chicken. My traitor mouth is watering.

If this were a day-in-the-life documentary, the food would be important. Worthy of a close-up. An image of the dysfunctional family as they tuck into a strange new dish, rife with symbolism.

Take Nanook's family, for example. They ate walrus. Although his family wasn't exactly his family. Apparently, his wife was away and some other woman filled in for the part on-screen. The filmmaker—a guy called Robert J. Flaherty—didn't have a strong grip on the whole documentary thing and the need for absolute truth. How could he, I guess, since his was the first one? Anyway, he fudged some stuff. Like Nanook's name wasn't Nanook. But Flaherty shot a whole bunch of film about the guy's life and called it *Nanook of the North*, and that's what everyone thinks of as the first documentary.

Once I take my first bite of paella, all thoughts of Nanook and documentary film and symbolism disappear like polar bears in a snowstorm. Paella's delicious.

I wish it sucked. I wish Sheri were the worst cook in Webster. No, in North America. But I can't stop eating. Soon, Dad and I are both leaning back in our chairs like overfed walruses.

Sheri gets up and takes our plates. In my endorphin-ridden

state, I decide that if she's going to cook like that and then do the dishes, I might change my whole opinion of her.

She runs a hand along Dad's cheek as she walks by him.

"We'll save dessert for later," she whispers. As if I'm not sitting right here.

I scrape my chair back. "I forgot I had to . . ."

My mind goes blank. I can't think of anything to say. My dad and Sheri both stare at me expectantly.

"I'm supposed to . . . go."

And then I barrel down the stairs because really, if I stay in that room, I'm going to throw up and that would be a waste of good paella.

I find myself leaning against the back of my closed bedroom door as if there's an armed invader in the house. And now that I think of it, there is. Sheri's an invader, and I think she's using those bazoombas as weapons on my dad. She must have quite the arsenal because otherwise, none of this makes sense. Sheri is *not* my dad's type. *Mom* was Dad's type—smart, insightful, and a hell of a lot more classy than that woman upstairs whose laugh I can still hear through this door.

That paella was a trick. I should never have tasted it.

As if I'm in a black-and-white film flashback with "15 months earlier" in sans serif across the bottom of the screen, I remember my dad's face during one of Mom's cancer treatments. There was a nurse there. Tracy. She didn't look much like a nurse. Even in her scrubs, Tracy seemed to have stepped out of a punk rock video. Black lipstick, heavy eyeliner, nose ring—Tracy was goth in a way that I'd only seen on TV. She was also quite . . . muscular.

"Built like a brick shit house" is how my dad described her. The same way he used to describe me. Except in Tracy's case, he didn't add, "and just as smart."

Strange or not, Tracy was my favorite nurse, and I think Mom liked her too. If you had questions, even hard questions, Tracy was the one to ask. She didn't flower around, making things sound sweeter than they were.

Tracy was the one who finally explained "stage 3" in a way that we understood. In Mom's case, it meant that the tumor in her pancreas had wrapped itself around a blood vessel. "Unresectable" meant they couldn't cut it out.

Mom was sitting in a reclining chair at the time, chemicals dripping into her arm. Dad and I were sitting on either side, in folding chairs. Mom seemed calm, as if Tracy were explaining something she already knew.

Dad looked like someone had cut open his jugular and drained the blood. After a minute, I had to look away. Graphic content. Some scenes are not suitable for all viewers.

I force my shoulders to relax. Sheri is a distraction. A rebound. A fling. And I should get out of the house, go for a drive, and clear my head.

What I need is distance. If I keep my distance and pretend Sheri doesn't exist, she will eventually disappear. Strippers must have strings of temporary relationships, right?

God, I hope I'm right.

chapter 9

a narrow escape from the cuckoo's nest

I start work at the cherry plant at the end of July. When Hannah picks me up after a twelve-hour shift, my hands are stained purple with cherry juice, I smell like a mixture of sweat and fruit punch, and my hair is molded into the shape of my hairnet. (Hairnets: absolutely humiliating. Not even James Dean could appear iconic in a hairnet.) It's only seven o'clock at night, but I'm dead tired. So tired that I fall asleep before we're halfway back to town.

"Hey." Hannah runs her fingernails lightly up my forearm until I pry my eyes open. "I've got something special planned for us, but I can take you home if you're too tired."

Home. Though that sounds tempting, so does the something

special. I sit up a little straighter. I've been hanging out with Hannah for more than a month now, with no real action. It's sort of like having a Porsche in your driveway and never turning the key.

I consider her lips for a moment. "Home. Um . . . no. Well, yes. How about home first for a shower? That will wake me up, and then we'll go out."

"Done." Her foot slips a bit as she hits the gas pedal, and she giggles. She's wearing black high-heeled shoes with strings that lace up her calves and a short denim skirt. I don't know if it would win any fashion awards, but it's more than enough to keep me awake for the rest of the drive.

I unlock the basement door and head straight for the shower without even checking to see if Dad's upstairs. When I come out, feeling less cherry-juice pink, Hannah's flipping through discs. She picks up *The Corporation*.

"That one's a bit heavy. It's all about proving that corporations are psycho."

She shoves it back on the shelf as if she's been caught snooping. "I know. I thought I was going to need antidepressants afterward."

"Seriously? You've seen it?"

She shrugs, blinks, flicks her hair over her shoulder. "You smell nice. You locked the bathroom door, though."

"Um . . . habit, I guess."

"Bad habit," she says, nuzzling against me.

"It will never happen again," I say. I'm thinking I may have stumbled into my own fantasy, and I'm just deciding whether or not I care that Dad may be upstairs when my phone rings and ruins it all. I make the mistake of glancing at it, and Lauren's number is lit up on the call display.

Flashing neon warning sign: Do not answer ex-girlfriend's call while hot new girl is in the room.

Apparently, I'm blind to neon. Or maybe two years of dating Lauren have ingrained me with Pavlov's-dog reflexes. I pick up the phone.

"Cole? Can you come over? I need to talk to you." After Hannah's low purr, Lauren's voice sounds young.

"Right now?" I scrub a hand through my hair.

"It's important. I need to see you."

I can tell she's upset, which makes me want to see her less. It's going to be messy.

I hang up the phone and wince at Hannah, feeling as if I've been called into battle.

"Lauren's upset about something. She says I have to stop by."

"Oh. Okay." Even though she looks disappointed, Hannah doesn't sound angry. Suddenly, all I want to do is blow off Lauren and hang out with the gorgeous girl standing in front of me, her teeth biting the corner of her lip, her eyebrows crinkled with the strain of thinking. The fact that she's not creating some big scene even though she had something planned . . .

"I'm sure it won't take long. I know it's not a great thing to ask, but you could wait and then we could hang out."

"Sure!" And Hannah's face is sunny again, as if there's never been a problem.

Ten minutes later we're parked on the street in front of Lauren's. We still have Hannah's car because she says she has her "surprise supplies" in the trunk.

"I'll be back as soon as I possibly can," I promise.

"No worries."

When I get to Lauren's door, I'm confused for a moment. For more than two years, I walked in without knocking. That doesn't seem right anymore, so I kind of knock and let myself in at the same time. Pepper, Lauren's little black poodle, goes crazy as soon as I enter, as if I'm his prodigal owner. When I scoop him up, he wiggles ecstatically in my arms.

"In here," Lauren calls, and I follow her voice to the living room. The curtains are pulled and the lamps are off, making it cavelike. Above the recliner hangs a giant cross-stitch, which reads: BE NOT FORGETFUL TO ENTERTAIN STRANGERS: FOR THEREBY SOME HAVE ENTERTAINED ANGELS UNAWARES. Above the words, there's a dour portrait of the Virgin Mary. Her righteous eyes follow me when I move. She's never seemed particularly hospitable, and tonight she's downright hostile.

I force myself to break the stare.

Lauren's curled in a corner of the couch with a cushion crushed against her chest. As soon as I put Pepper down, he runs to lie on Lauren's bare feet.

"What's up?" I admit, I'm tempted to copy the poodle. It's impossible to date someone for that long and not want to hug her when she's upset, maybe put my hand in her hair and tell her everything's going to be okay. It must be some sort of programmed male instinct. Or I was a poodle in a past life.

I resist. I stay standing and remind myself of who's waiting for me outside. Lauren and I are over. She's about to tell me that she wants to get back together, and I'm going to tell her—as nicely as I can because I *do* care for Lauren—that we can't have the *Princess Bride* ending. It's just not going to happen. Her life is going to be a fairy tale and my life . . . well, lately it's more like a Martin Scorsese film. The two just don't mix.

"I need to talk to you about . . ." She starts, stumbles, and starts again. "First of all, I wanted to say that I miss you. Do you ever feel that way?"

"Sometimes," I hedge.

"Do you remember our last afternoon together, when I came by your house?" she says.

"Yeah." Maybe it wasn't the best idea to sleep together that day, but it was a damn good hangover cure.

"Why are you staring like that?"

I forgot how well she knows me. "I was just thinking . . . that was a nice dress."

Lauren half grins, and I smirk. My shoulders relax. Even though I still don't know exactly why I'm here, at least I'm seeing the real Lauren. My Lauren. I have to admit, I've missed her.

Lauren's family moved from Alberta when we were in second grade, and we grew up one block apart. She lived on Juniper Street and I lived on Pine.

I remember when I met her. I was in the playground with Greg before school (friends don't change much in a town like Webster), and a scrawny little girl was swinging on our monkey bars.

"Hey, *we're* playing here," I said, or something to that effect.

Greg elbowed me. "Be nice to her or she'll tell Mr. Green. She's in our class."

"She is not in our class. She's too little," I said.

Greg just shrugged, the same don't-say-I-didn't-warn-you type of shrug he would still be giving me a decade later.

I don't know who ended up playing on the monkey bars, but I know that Greg was right about Lauren being in our class. There she was in the center row when I walked in.

I ignored her for the rest of that year and the year after that, pretty much right up until Trisha Bernard's seventh-grade birthday party, when the bottle spun and pointed to me. Lauren and I were shoved into a dark closet together. I kissed her, the fastest kiss in the history of the world, and then I ignored her for another two years until I saw her at the ninth-grade Christmas dance.

I don't know how or when it happened, but suddenly she was cute. Thin and blond and shiny, Lauren was exactly how the girl next door always looks in the movies. Her scrawny calves had become long, shapely legs, and she was wearing this glittery pink lip stuff that made her mouth look like a Christmas ornament.

It took me three songs to get up the courage to ask Lauren to dance. When it turned out to be a slow dance, I spent the entire time wondering if she could feel what was going on in my pants. And if she could, was that a good thing or a bad thing?

Hannah. I have to remember Hannah's outside. I glance at the front window.

Lauren stands up and straightens her shoulders as if she's about to do a public presentation. "Cole, before we talk about what I wanted to talk to you about, could you just think about that day for a minute and tell me . . . well, tell me whether you think—when you remember that day—if we could have something together again."

There it is. It's not fair, really. Breaking up with her the first time was hard enough. Why does she need me to say those things again? "Lauren, I'm—"

"I know I did some things wrong."

For Lauren to say that is unusual. She lives in a world where mistakes don't happen. Maybe it's because her dad's an accountant. And he's old, at least sixty. Which is probably why her parents are so overprotective.

"Greg said something recently," she continues. "He made me think I wasn't, you know, supportive in the way I could have been."

"You were always supportive," I say. How many times did the two of us sit by my mom's hospital bed, watching Mom sleep or spooning ice chips to her one by one? Lauren was like a butterfly in that room—a splash of color fluttering across a sterile white screen.

I feel like crap. What kind of person doesn't like butterflies?

"No. Greg's right," she says. "I should have talked to you more about the future, and about the things you wanted. But we had a lot of good times too, and . . ."

Damn Greg. I glance toward the window again, imagining Hannah sitting in the car, wondering what in the world I'm dealing with in here.

Following my gaze, Lauren walks to the window and flicks

open the curtain a little. When she turns back to me, her face has changed. Her lips are pressed tightly together, and her eyes are like cut stones. She is the un-butterfly.

"You came here with *Hannah*?"

I look away. The Virgin Mary glares at me from the wall.

"This is why we broke up!" I want to yell at her, or the Virgin Mary, or both. "I can't do the right thing all the time." Although logically, I can't see what's so wrong about coming with Hannah. Lauren and I are not together. Hannah and I have plans. Besides, I thought after I gave her a ride home with her groceries, we were on our way to being friends again.

Judging by the look on Lauren's face, I was mistaken.

I make one last attempt. "You called at the last minute. We were together."

"Is that all you think of me? That I'm an errand to run while your new girlfriend waits in the car?"

Put it that way and I can see why Lauren might be mad. But really, I'm too tired to deal with this sort of argument. The kind that's not even about what it's pretending to be about. After work, I had wanted to go home and sleep. Now I want to go somewhere with Hannah. I definitely don't want to be here.

"Hannah's not here to hurt your feelings. She's here because we were going out. Then, when *you* called, I made an effort to change my plans to see what *you* needed."

"How considerate."

"You're making a big deal out of nothing. She's a friend."

Lauren sniffs. "You know she spends all her time making 'friends' with guys because the girls think she's a slut, right?" Then, immediately: "That was mean. I take it back. But not the rest."

"Do you actually need something?" If this were a courtroom, I would want it officially noted that I *tried* to be understanding.

She answers with her teeth clenched together. "No. I don't need anything from you, and I never will need anything from someone who can break up with one girl and start screwing another the week after."

"I didn't screw anyone a week after breaking up with you." Fondled, yes. Screwed, no. There's a difference.

"Oh, so you're just screwing her *now*. That's way better." The poodle whimpers from the couch.

"I'm not screwing Hannah!" Not that I want to be discussing this with Lauren. Why am I telling her this?

"Like I believe that! Just get out of my house!" By the end of her sentence, she's pushing me, both hands open against my chest, across the room.

I escape out the door, wincing as it slams behind me. Then I climb back into Hannah's car like Clint Eastwood paddling away from Alcatraz.

"Everything okay?" Hannah asks.

Taking a deep breath, I try to figure out what just happened. That was a seriously warped, misguided attempt to get back together.

"Is everything okay? I suppose that depends on whether you think crazy is okay," I say.

"Are *you* okay?"

Why does nobody else ever think to ask that? I smile at her. "I'm okay."

She pulls away from the curb and we drive in silence for a few minutes, heading out of town. I have to take a few deep breaths to smooth the tangled mess of fishing line that my brain has become. On one hand, I feel bad about leaving Lauren so upset. I'm the one who broke up with her after two years. Of course she's emotional. Girls get emotional. I should have been more patient. I have this nagging feeling she was trying to say something important and I ruined her moment.

On the other hand, let's be honest. The girl was freaking out. Being patient in the face of crazy doesn't come easily to me. And Lauren has to figure out, eventually, that I'm not the one for her. I don't belong in that cloistered living room. I need bigger spaces. Spaces where the Virgin Mary isn't watching me from the wall.

There is no right answer. No immediate way to untangle the situation. While my brain goes into neural overload trying to figure out where I went wrong, I find myself staring at Hannah's legs again.

I reach over to touch the warm skin at the edge of her skirt, and she glances from the road to smile at me.

"Where exactly are you taking us?"

"Nester," she says.

"Nester?"

"Relax," she says. "You'll like it."

chapter 10

sausages, all varieties

I raise an eyebrow at Hannah. Nester's one of the farming districts on the outskirts of town and there's not much there, unless you count cows. Or a small polygamous group. (Seriously.) Or more cows.

But I've forgotten about the fairgrounds, and that's where Hannah pulls in, the headlights sweeping swaths of light through the long brown grass as the car bumps off the pavement and onto the field. Once she cuts the engine, it's almost completely dark. Above us, there are so many stars that the sky doesn't look quite real. We could be in another country, populated only by frogs and crickets.

If this were an alien flick, this is when we'd get abducted.

"C'mon," Hannah says, so I follow her to the trunk and she passes me a flashlight, a blanket, and a backpack. Then she picks her way toward the bandstand, where the announcers call the action during the annual demolition derby. That's when drivers with rusted-out beaters try to sideswipe other drivers with rusted-out beaters and the one with the better beater wins the prize. The derby's the only other time I've ever been here.

Hannah uses her own flashlight to guide us up the bandstand stairs. Then she tugs the blanket from me and spreads it on the stage. The backpack yields a thermos of spiked hot chocolate along with crackers, cheese, chocolate, and three kinds of sausage.

"Wow. You know how to pack a picnic."

"Thanks," she says, settling herself in the middle of the bounty.

"Have you done this before?"

"What kind of question is that? This night is all for you, Cole."

We don't get to the snacks right away.

The evening air has finally started to cool. A tiny breeze moves over us as Hannah's lips trace hot circles down my neck to the base of my throat. Beneath the blanket, I can feel the warped slats of the wooden floor. In the space between the railings and the roof, small bat shapes swoop. Hannah puts her hand on my thigh and her lips on my ear and then, because I can't let her keep taking charge all the time, I get up on my knees and tug off her shirt, then I toss my jean jacket and T-shirt to the side.

I have this thing about girls with long hair, preferably with their shirts off. It's probably from some cinematic sex scene that got burned into my brain. Anyway, Hannah's hair is long. And now her shirt is off. In the almost-perfect dark of the bandstand, her skin glows faintly and her eyes glisten. Not that I'm looking at her eyes. She slides down beneath me and reaches up to draw me closer and for a few minutes, I can't remember where we are, or how we got here, or even my name.

A while later, though, she's tugging at my boxers with her teeth.

I've lost focus.

In my mind, every guy I know is screaming that I'm an idiot. I *am* an idiot. No question. Here's the problem: I can't get Lauren out of my head. Just as Hannah's tongue is tracing my waistband, I get a flash of Lauren sitting on her couch, arms wrapped around herself as if she's trying to keep her insides in place. As Hannah's breath creates a circle of heat against my skin, I hear the hurt in Lauren's voice after she realizes there's another girl in the idling car outside.

Lauren and I broke up. That was a good decision. Whether or not there are hurt feelings, I did the right thing. You'd think that knowledge would make me immune to moments like this.

Apparently not.

"Wait," I whisper to Hannah as her mouth slides downward. Then I have to resist banging my head against the wooden floor because who in his right mind says "wait" to Hannah Deprez?

Thankfully, Hannah thinks I'm being a gentleman.

"That's sweet," she says. "Not necessary, but sweet."

"Next time," I say into her neck.

It takes a while for my breathing to become normal again and my red blood cells to return to their rightful routes. Eventually, we haul ourselves up to sit cross-legged and I turn on the flashlight, standing it on end like a lantern. Hot chocolate and garlic sausage go together surprisingly well, I discover. This girl knows how to choose food.

I find myself gazing at Hannah as she pours a fresh cup from the thermos. A wisp of steam seems to glow in the dark as it floats past her cheekbone. I'm thinking again about the things that Lauren said.

"How come you don't get along with the other girls in our class?" I ask.

Her eyes remain on the hot chocolate. "We get along," she says.

"You don't hang out."

Glancing up through her eyelashes, the look she gives me is assessing. It's the quick, perceptive look of the spy femme fatale in a James Bond movie. It's not the look of a bimbo.

"How come you pretend to be so . . ." I search for something less offensive than ditzy, or flighty, or dumb. ". . . focused on fun all the time," I finish, "when you're actually smart?"

She laughs a little. "It's a tough crowd here."

"Who's a tough crowd?"

"Everyone. You've all known each other forever. The girls decided I was a slut as soon as I got here. Dallas was really the only one who was nice to me, for months. And then everyone said I was sleeping with him."

I blink. It never occurred to me that Hannah *hadn't* slept with Dallas.

"Hang on," I say. "Hold that thought." I pull my jacket off the floor and scrabble through the pockets until I find my camera. Framing Hannah's silhouette in the viewfinder, I press record. Her dark hair blends into the background of bandstand boards and night sky, her pale face floating.

"All right," I say. "Tell me what you've experienced of Webster."

"The real story?" She smiles. "Are you sure?"

"Completely."

"You're not going to post it online, right?"

"I promise. No local viewers."

"Here's the reality, then. One on one, the girls around here are okay. In a group, they're vipers."

I laugh at the exaggeration, trying not to shake the camera.

Hannah nods, wide eyed. "I'm serious. You should be glad you're a guy."

"Guys are easier?" What am I saying? Of course we are.

"Yeah." She smiles. "You're easy."

"Great. So you're hanging around with me because I'm easy."

"Are you complaining?"

"No complaints." In fact, everyone should have such simple reasons for hanging around with me. "Tell me more, though. Tell me what it's like to move here."

"Dallas and I have talked about that," she says. "We're the new kids. You guys all know each other. You know who peed on the teeter-totter in kindergarten and whose dad slept with the receptionist at the dentist's office, and you know the entire dating history of every single high school student."

This is true.

On the view screen, I watch the way she squares her shoulders. I wish I had a professional-style reflector so I could soften the flashlight beam on her skin.

"You're not used to explaining yourselves," she says. "And

you don't ask others questions because you're not used to having to work to understand them. Maybe you *want* to build friendships with new people, but everyone in town already gets you, so you haven't learned how to reach that stage with a stranger."

I wince a little at that one. Because she's right. I've been spending time with Hannah for weeks, and I barely understand who she is. Is she right about the whole theory of small-town relationships too? Thinking about it makes my head feel overstuffed. This is deeper than I expected from Hannah.

"I admit," I say, "you're more complicated than I thought."

She smiles.

Then a clear thought crystalizes. "The rest of us only *think* we understand each other. We change. Or at least some of us change."

"And everyone else goes on assuming you're still the same," she says.

I nod. "Exactly."

"Sometimes," Hannah says, ruining my shot by moving to lean against me in the dark, "it just feels good to have people you can talk to, you know?"

It's surprisingly similar to what I thought my mom would say—the mom of my imagination who was cutting onions in the kitchen a few weeks ago. *When you break up, you lose the person you tell things to.*

Which is what I'm supposed to be doing, according to my new life plan. I need to cut people loose, not start relationships.

I put down the camera.

"I'm worried that I might become the person you talk to, and you might become the person I talk to, and then I'll leave for Vancouver next year and everything will be complicated," I tell Hannah.

There must be something about this bandstand that heightens communication skills. I've been spilling my guts here.

"I just ended things with Lauren," I continue. "I don't want to start anything that could become . . . messy."

"It will only be messy if we make it messy." Hannah's smile is back in place, and when she looks up at me through her eyelashes, my resolutions melt a little.

"We don't have to worry about the rest of the year or leaving town," she says. "We've got lots of nights left this summer."

It's more of a question than a statement.

Apparently, my communication skills were temporary. I can't figure out how to respond. It's possible that one of Greg's little green aliens has beamed itself inside my skull. He's banging his tiny green fist on my cranium and shouting that getting attached is not only a bad idea, it's downright dangerous. He's saying something about film school, and Uganda, and people always leaving you, so why the hell bother, and . . .

It's difficult to give the alien my full attention because Hannah is kissing me again. Then she is doing other things. In one last burst of concentration, I manage to hear the green man say something about wooden bandstand floors and splinters in my ass. But who the hell cares about splinters when Hannah's body is pressed along the length of mine?

Sunday is the one-year anniversary of my mom's death. I haven't told anyone this. I suppose if I'd told Hannah when we were in Nester, she could have squished my head against her breasts and made sympathetic noises. Or if I'd told Greg, he could have gotten me mercilessly drunk.

Neither of those options seemed quite right. Weirdly enough, I've been wanting to call Lauren. I suppose it's because she spent all those hours with me at the hospital. That's the trouble, though. When we left the hospital, she was the same person and I wasn't.

So I can't call my emotionally unstable ex-girlfriend.

I need another option.

I decide that the times I've felt closest to Mom—since she died, I mean—they all had to do with food. So in her honor, I'm going to cook.

From the shelf above the fridge, I pull down the cookbook that looks most worn, thinking the creased cover might indicate commonly cooked recipes. And it does. Almost every page has food splattered on it, or a bent corner, or a note saying "not so much sugar" or "good if you add chicken." It feels strange to read my mom's handwriting. It's like thinking I see her in a crowd when she's not really there.

Some of the recipes in here are familiar to me, like Hunter's Chicken and Seafood Pot Pie. Others are completely foreign: Chicken Tangine. The recipe introduction says it's a Moroccan favorite. There's no picture, so I can't tell if I've ever eaten it. I pass it by, eventually. It reminds me too much of Sheri's paella.

Finally, I come to a recipe that Mom marked "super easy." There's even a bracket she drew around most of the ingredients with a scribbled "just use spaghetti sauce." We have spaghetti sauce in the cupboard. By some miracle, we have the other two ingredients too: a can of chickpeas and a tray of breakfast sausages. The recipe says Italian sausages, but I figure they can't be too different.

I'm supposed to stir together the tomato sauce and the chickpeas and put the sausages on top. Super easy, just like the note says. I run my fingers across her words. I can see her face. I can see the way she would smile with one corner of her lips higher than the other, brushing her bangs out of her eyes.

The real introduction to the recipe says, "Every cook needs a weeknight standby. Something you can throw together when the day gets away from you." Or when life gets away from you.

The sausage dish goes in the oven for forty minutes. The recipe says thirty, but Mom crossed it out. "Depends on the size of the sausages," she wrote.

"Doesn't everything." My dad would grin as he squeezed into the kitchen to check out the action.

"Gross. I'm in the house, you know." That would be my eleven- or twelve-year-old self. I can see the whole scene, choppy as if it were edited the old-fashioned way, with a sharp pair of scissors.

When I was little, before I even started kindergarten, Mom and Dad lived in an A-frame on the outskirts of town. Seriously. An A-frame. I vaguely remember it. I remember dark, paneled walls. I remember the huge vegetable garden in the backyard. And I remember the corduroy pants that Mom sewed for me, the ones that were two sizes too big and made terrible swooshing sounds with every step.

They must have been going through a back-to-the-land phase. It seems kind of romantic when I think of it. Were they romantic, or am I pulling my memories from bad seventies films? I rack my brain for examples. I remember them holding hands, window shopping. They went out to dinner every year on their anniversary. Does that count?

Then there was the hospital, of course. Once Dad drove to

Burger Barn just as they were closing and convinced them to reopen to make Mom a chocolate milk shake because she wasn't eating and for some reason he thought a chocolate milk shake might solve all her problems.

Supposedly, smell is the sense most strongly linked to memory. Maybe that's why, as the sausages heat up, I'm wondering about my parents' marriage. Were they in love, still? I think they were. Then again, I'm basing my conclusions on a chocolate milk shake.

It's not exactly something I can ask Dad. Even if I managed to spit out the question, I can't imagine him coming up with a coherent answer.

"Course I loved her. What the hell kinda question is that?" he'd say.

The sausages are delicious when they're done. Crispy on top with the sauce thick and rich below them. I leave the dish bubbling on the counter while I boil noodles, and then I kind of hang around and wait for Dad to get home. I guess I'm fishing for a repeat of his chicken dinner reaction.

Eventually, I stop waiting. He's probably out with Sheri.

I eat my half by myself in front of the TV, and I forget to notice how it tastes. Then I stumble downstairs and crawl into bed.

• • •

In the middle of the night, I have to pee. I drag myself from under the covers.

"Oh, baby . . ."

I hear the words faintly, but they're enough to freeze me in place, one foot on the threshold of the bathroom and one in the air. My bathroom is directly below the upstairs bathroom and the upstairs bathroom is right next to Dad's bedroom and there's a big vent in between.

I don't know whether to go forward or backward. It's past midnight and I really have to pee. It's possible I imagined that voice.

"Oh my God, baby . . ."

Backward. I definitely need to go backward. Because unless my dad is watching porn in his bedroom—and he doesn't have a TV in his bedroom—then what I am hearing is Sheri. . . .

"Yes!"

Backward. Must retreat. Quickly and quietly.

I scuttle to my room and pull the door firmly shut. Then I fling myself onto the bed and pull two pillows and all my blankets over my head. It's possible I should leave the house entirely, go for a middle-of-the-night walk. Of course, if I do that, I might have to keep walking until I get to the coast because I really, really don't want to go upstairs in my house ever again.

I imagine describing the scene to Greg.

"Oh, fuck," he'd say, wincing and grinning at the same time.

"Literally. Have you ever heard it when your parents—?"

"That's disgusting," he'd reply.

I'd shudder.

"I feel like I just took the lid off the garbage can and a pack of rats jumped out. And now I don't want to take the garbage out. For a year."

"A decade, at least," he'd tell me.

That's what he'd say if I told him. But somehow, I know I'm not going to tell him. This is just too . . . wrong. If I tell him, it'll be like actually admitting that everything's going to hell.

chapter 11

what ripe peaches and reputations have in common

Hannah's working at a fruit stand on the highway for the summer, selling ripe peaches to sweaty tourists who've been stuck in their SUVs for too long. In my opinion, every man to stop at that particular fruit stand is going to drive away with ripe peaches on his mind and it's going to have nothing to do with the actual produce.

When Hannah's finished, with peaches and with high school, she'll study anthropology at the University of BC. Apparently she's signed up for the biology, chemistry, and math pre-reqs this year.

"Whoa! Did you take all sciences last year too?" We're in my bedroom, where I'm sprawled on the bed. I'm sort of hoping

Hannah will join me, but she hasn't shown any signs of that.

"Well, I wasn't in your artsy-fartsy comparative civilization class, was I? Where did you think I was, Cole? Remedial?"

That's uncomfortably close to what I *did* think, at least until a few weeks ago. I cover quickly. "You're going to wind up shaking the principal's hand at graduation as he gives you the plaque for best academic performance."

As I say the words, I remember that was one of Lauren's goals. Top academic student, full scholarship to the university of her choice, major in elementary education.

"I wouldn't accept the plaque," Hannah says, rolling her eyes in a way that might be serious or might be joking. "It'd ruin my reputation."

We're having this conversation because Hannah found the Vancouver Film Studio brochure in my room.

She's not even supposed to be here. One of the mental guidelines I've devised in my keep-it-casual rule book is that daytime dates are off-limits. Boyfriends and girlfriends do things during the day. People in noncommitted relationships get together only at night.

But she turned up at my door this morning, and there was no one else home. I thought it might be entertaining—just this once—to let her in. I didn't think we'd be talking about film school.

"Where did you get this, anyway?" she asks, flipping through the pages, examining the pictures of black-shirted, would-be directors peering through their camera lenses.

"Ms. Gladwell."

"Wow. This is pretty creative for the counseling department. You sure you don't want to be an electrician?" She thins her lips and raises her pitch in an impressive Ms. Gladwell impression. "Good money in the trades these days."

I burst out laughing. "She wanted you to be an electrician? She wanted me to be a plumber."

"Oh, no." Hannah shakes her head. "Electrical was for Dallas. I'm supposed to go to a university. She's all about female empowerment."

"Ms. Gladwell? She didn't strike me as particularly empowered."

"You're getting me off topic. Is this why you've been filming things?" She waves the brochure under my nose.

It does something, that brochure. It gives me a prickle of excitement. The same kind I felt on that night when Greg first told me that Hannah Deprez thought I was hot.

I nod. "I'm making a short documentary for my application."

"What's it about?"

"About the Web as an actual web and about people getting stuck here, even though they dream about leaving. You know, trapped because of their families, or their jobs, or lack of money. It's hard to explain." It's too vague to explain, really, too unfinished. If I try to outline my ideas in words, they might vanish.

"I have time," Hannah says, finally plunking herself on the edge of the bed.

"Okay. But not right now," I say. I pull her on top of me. "Unless you want to film this."

We are mostly naked and slicked with sweat when Hannah props herself on an elbow. I can barely speak, and I'm pretty sure my bones have turned gelatinous. Whatever just happened to me, it was good. If summer ended right now, it would all have been worth it.

This is the problem with Hannah. She's amazing. And not just in bed. She's unexpectedly sharp. She makes me laugh. If I'm not careful, I'm going to end up liking her a little too much.

"How come we hang out at your house, but I've never met your dad?" Hannah asks.

Case in point. People in casual relationships do not meet parents. I raise my head from the mattress and look her up and down. "Like this?"

"Idiot." She pummels me with a pillow. "Assuming I had all my clothes on, wouldn't he want to meet me?"

"Why are we talking about parents?"

"I'm serious. Would he disapprove of me?"

"My dad? He'd think you're hot."

"Excellent." She smiles like a satisfied cat. "I'll come over for dinner, then. I'll bring something. Cookies? What would he like?"

There are warning lights flashing in my head. "You can't come over for dinner. Our kitchen's disgusting. You'll stop hanging out with me, fearful you'll contract a rare contagious disease."

Hannah laughs. "Cole, you *are* a contagious disease."

This is bad. In the words of Tom Hanks: Houston, we have a problem.

"Or you could come to my place instead," she adds.

Hannah's rich. Her dad's some sort of ex-foreign-service guy who retired early. Their house is on a hillside on the west edge of town, looking down over the fields and the river.

"You live in a mansion. I can't go inside that place. I'll track mud on the marble floors or something."

She rolls her eyes. "Not likely. But my mom will smother you. She'll offer you tea or juice or milk and date squares, and then she'll do something excruciating like get out a picture of me in my ballet tutu when I was three."

"Can you just bring me the baked goods and the tutu picture and skip the parent meeting?"

Meeting a girl's parents simply doesn't mesh with "summer fling." I've been working hard here so neither one of us gets the wrong idea. She is not helping.

She whaps me with the pillow again. "You can't see the tutu picture."

"I'll just take the squares, then. I like date squares."

"Stop trying to change the subject. When do I meet your family?"

"If I *had* a family, I suppose you could meet them. What I *have* is a disaster, so how about we forget that part?"

The words come out more bitter than I meant them to. Hannah's smile fades, and her eyes grow soft and sympathetic. I can't take it. I'm not some puppy who needs rescuing from the pound.

"We should do something," I say, pulling myself off the bed.

"Okay." Thankfully, she follows my lead. "It's gorgeous out."

We have our clothes back on when I hear the front door open and footsteps upstairs.

"Is that your dad?" Hannah asks.

But there are two voices.

"We should go out," I say. "Where do you want to go?"

"Somewhere we haven't been yet. Somewhere interesting." She's still rubbing my arm, as if she needs to soothe me.

I step away, search the dresser top for my wallet. "Agreed. Let's blow this place."

Upstairs, Sheri's laugh clangs. I need to get out, preferably with the speed of an instant transporter.

"Let's go across the border to Idaho and buy pork rinds and then drive as far as we can before dark," I say.

"Pork rinds?" She's standing in front of my mirror, smoothing her hair into a ponytail. Her nose wrinkles.

"Whatever you want. You can buy six billion kinds of junk food there cheaper than here."

"Let's go hiking," she says in the same eager voice Lauren would have used to suggest shopping. "My dad just gave me a trail guide."

I'm not sure hiking sounds better than shopping. Marginally, I suppose. It definitely doesn't sound better than pork rinds.

"Hiking?" I can practically taste the salty, fatty pork deliciousness dissolving on my tongue.

Sheri laughs. Again. When did my dad get so funny?

"You'll love it," Hannah says.

So I agree. At least I'll be out of the house.

An hour later, we're grinding our way up Mount Slando, picking through the subalpine meadows where layers of moss and hot pink fireweed cover the wide patches between scraggly evergreens.

"I don't see any bears!" Hannah says cheerfully.

No bears along the edges of the trees and none in the dusty grizzly wallow we pass. There are no bears because it's too freaking hot and the freaking bears are freaking smart enough to be napping in the freaking shade like civilized creatures.

We reach the end of the wildflowers. From here, the peak stretches up in great jagged slabs of scree.

"It's like a giant-size pile of broken crackers," Hannah remarks.

I think mournfully of pork rinds.

As she climbs the first slab, Hannah peels off her top to reveal her hot pink sports bra.

Still not measuring up to deep-fried goodness. "You should keep your shirt on," I grumble. "Your arms are going to get scraped on the rock."

She turns to raise an eyebrow at me. I know that look.

Slowly, she peels off her bra.

Then she flings it downhill, along with her shirt.

And now Hannah is balancing topless across the first slab, like some genetic mash up of an Amazon warrior and an insane ballerina.

"Coming?" she calls.

I've lost the ability to speak.

"You're not shy, are you?" she teases.

Well, I've been busy ogling her breasts. Now that she's mentioned it, this could become an embarrassing situation.

"What if someone's up there?"

"Who would be up there?"

And of course she's right. Everyone else, including the bears, is bound to be smarter than us. Didn't I agree to come because I wouldn't have to interact with other human beings? Plus, I'm not the one who's going to be embarrassed. I hastily strip off my shirt, grab my water bottle, and leap over the first few rocks to catch up.

We're not exactly a pretty sight. I mean, there are good views, like Hannah turning to smile back at me, the sun bouncing off her so brightly I can almost see the lens flare. And then there are the bad, like me losing my balance halfway between boulders and winding up with one hand and one foot on the downhill rock and one hand and one foot on the uphill rock, my butt in the air like a big slapstick comedy target.

"This is ridiculous," I grouch.

"That's what it's all about." Hannah shouts, then waits to hear the echo.

"It's all about what?" Screw the echo.

"It's about being ridiculous on a day off with no one in the world to care."

We collapse at the summit, on a slab of rock that's flat and gray like a giant cookie sheet. The sun beats down on us until my skin crackles, but I don't care. I'm too hot and too tired to move.

Just by turning my head to the side, I can see the perfectly blue lake below us and the peaks encircling the sky in every direction. Peak after peak after peak. It's like getting aerial footage without the helicopter.

"Can you imagine if you were one of those explorer guys and you climbed up here?" I ask. "What if you were trying to scope a route and all you saw in every direction was more mountains? That would be seriously depressing."

"They followed the rivers," Hannah says. She's stretched out on her stomach. There are white bands across the skin of her back where her bathing suit would usually be. She has a sheen of sweat on her shoulders. It would be seriously sexy if I weren't too tired to move.

"It was David Thompson," Hannah says after the sun has baked our brains for a while longer.

"What was?"

"Your explorer. He was the first white guy through here. We talked about him in history last year, remember?"

"Did he find what he was looking for?"

"He got all the way to the coast."

All the way to the coast. I look down at the blue and try to trace it west, but my eyes are stopped by rock and forest before they get anywhere.

"So explain to me why we're up on this rock? We should be down there paddling."

"Are you kidding?" she says. I can barely move, but somehow Hannah scrambles up. "This hike was for posterity, baby."

"Posterior?" I check out her ass as she walks a few steps to the waist-high stone cairn on the peak. Confidently, she pulls a few rocks from the marker and reaches inside. When her hand emerges, she's clutching a small canister.

"Posterity, you idiot. Not posterior."

"What have you got?"

"A logbook," she says, shaking a yellowed notepad out of the canister. "The guidebook said it would be here."

Sitting down and flipping the log open on her bent knees, she scribbles something and passes it to me. Underneath the date, she's written

First Topless Ascent of Mount Slando
Hannah Deprez and Cole Owens

I'm laughing when I hand it back. But I'm uncomfortable, too. I feel as if I've been engraved on this place, the same way the rocks have etched themselves into my calves. I feel as if I've signed in when I really, really wanted today to be all about checking out.

"You could come to my place for dinner tonight," Hannah says quietly. "If you want to."

I'd rather follow David Thompson down the river.

"I should work on my film," I tell her. Which is obviously the most lame excuse ever but the best I can do on short notice. When I look at Hannah, glowing and half-naked, I understand how people get stuck in this town permanently. They meet a great girl, get a job at the mill, buy a bungalow, drive a mini-van, retire at the old-folks home, and end up in Valley View Cemetery.

This can't happen.

"I have to get some more footage so I can start editing."

"Sure," she says. "Another time."

And we start downhill, back toward the bungalows and minivans.

chapter 12

doors versus windows

I don't actually intend to do any filming today, but I bump into Tracy, my mom's nurse, at the strip mall late in the afternoon. I'm trying to buy aloe cream for my back, which is as fried and blistered as the pork rinds I never ate thanks to Hannah.

When I see Tracy, I figure it's serendipity—a great subject, standing in front of a perfectly kitschy strip mall. Grocery store, health food store, coffee shop, and dry cleaner's. It's not quite as perfect as the gingerbread bakery backdrop I used for Greg's interview, but it has the same small-town feel to it.

Tracy eyes my camera warily, as if I might ask her to dance or break into song.

"It will be painless. I promise," I tell her.

"It's a good thing you're cute," she says finally.

Ignoring that, I set up the camera. I've been trying to remember the rule of thirds lately—things slightly off center carry more inherent tension. With Tracy a little to the right and the windows and signs of the stores extending off to the left, it seems to work.

"Okay. Let's start with an easy one. How long have you lived in the Web?" I ask.

"Two years," she says. Which is perfect. As a relative newcomer, she'll have objective opinions about this place.

"What made you move here?"

"A job offer, mostly," she says. "And I wanted a place where I could have a house, a dog, and a big vegetable garden."

Tracy doesn't seem like the vegetable garden type. On a scale of one to ten, where one is "grows organic produce" and ten is "eats baked beans out of the can," I would have pegged Tracy at a nine, at least.

"Since you've been here, has it met your expectations?"

She smiles. I don't know if I've ever seen Tracy really smile before. There've been sympathetic half smiles in the hospital. Bedside-manner smiles. But not a real, cheek-stretching, eye-crinkling smile like this one.

"It has far exceeded my expectations."

This is not helpful, project-wise. Scrapping the rule of thirds,

I focus her squarely in the center of the screen, as if that will force the truth from her.

"How? How has it exceeded them?"

"It's more open than I thought," she says. "You worry that people will be narrow-minded in a small place, but I haven't found that at all. I fell in love. And my neighbor—even though she's about a hundred years old—she's teaching me how to grow biodynamic blueberries."

"Biodynamic blueberries," I repeat.

"I know!"

I lower the camera. This is completely useless. Still, I can't help feeling good for Tracy. I mean, she looks so damned happy.

"So you fell in love with the town or with a person?"

"Both!" She beams.

"Well. Congratulations."

When she walks away, she takes her bubble of levity with her and leaves me feeling tired. Making this film is going to require some less chipper characters. It's as if everyone around me is living on a *Sound of Music* set, wearing green curtain dresses and singing in trees. Do I have to be the one to tell them that life can go downhill, faster than that Nazi kid can blow his whistle?

When I started this project, I thought there were plenty of people in Webster wishing they could escape. It turns out I might be the only one.

I shove my camera deep in my pocket and push into the drugstore in search of my aloe. If I'm alone in this feeling, that's fine. It will make it easier to leave them all behind. Everything according to plan.

On the Saturday after school starts, there's supposed to be a massive party at the gravel pits. Hannah's picking me up.

"Dad? Are you listening to me? I'm heading out."

Parked in the recliner, Dad's focused on the TV. He's watching a doc about Gulf War syndrome.

"I'm going out."

When he still doesn't respond, I plant myself between his chair and the screen.

"You look more like a door than a window," he mumbles, taking a pull of his beer and leaning around me to see.

"I'll be back late." I move slightly to the side.

He belches.

"Are you okay?" He and I aren't warm and fuzzy types, but this level of conversation is especially lame. It strikes me that for someone who's into nonfiction, like me, Dad doesn't seem too interested in dealing with reality these days.

"Fine. Fine. Get out of here." Dad waves his beer in the direction of the door. Then he hoists himself out of the chair, presumably to get himself another bottle. He doesn't fold down the footrest of the recliner, and as he tries to swing his leg over the top of it, his foot doesn't clear the upholstery. He hops a couple times. I lean over, trying to help, but I'm too far away and the chair's between us. He lands sprawled on the floor, groaning. On the television, a scientist describes how experimental vaccines and chemical contamination may have affected the brains of Gulf War soldiers.

"Are you all right?" I kneel beside him.

"Son of a . . ."

This close, I can smell the fumes coming off him, a stench like Dallas's living room on a Sunday morning.

"Are you drunk?"

"No, I'm not drunk," Dad says as he hauls himself to a sitting position. The unsteady swoon of his head atop his neck says otherwise.

"How about I make a pot of coffee before I go?"

"Gone, Cole." He shifts to lean heavily against me. Which is bad for the survival of my clean shirt. Good, in that I can no longer see his face and I have a sinking feeling that my dad might actually be crying.

"She's gone," he says.

And then I get it. It happens to me too. The sudden, acute awareness of Mom's absence. On TV, the narrator explains armor-piercing uranium. This is like armor-piercing grief.

They don't warn you about it when they explain the stages of loss. My aunt, for example, said the stages were anger, and shock, and some sort of bargaining with God. "Unforeseen periods of mental collapse" wasn't on the list.

I pat Dad's back in sympathy.

"She's gone to work the Okanagan circuit. They move around, you know . . . the dancers. People get tired of seeing the same bodies, so they switch towns. She's been able to stay at her cousin's house until now. . . ."

My whole body turns cold.

It's Sheri. Dad's crying over Sheri.

I shove him off my chest and scramble to my feet. Then I smooth my shirt, checking for snot. I'm clear.

"I have to go."

No response.

"You just grab yourself another beer."

He doesn't reply. I leave him staring at the carpet and, with the sounds of falling bombs in the background, slam the door behind me.

chapter 13

ditch sitting:
the original version

I'm trapped at a gravel pit party with a bunch of people I don't want to see.

I'm ignoring them. All of them. In front of me, a bonfire sends sparks swirling and swarming like living creatures, so bright they seem certain to last forever. Or drift into the pine branches and ignite. Or spiral into the stratosphere. Except every time I think one is going to make it, it's extinguished.

"'Extinguished' is an ugly word." I say this to the guy in the red plaid jacket and foam-front baseball cap who's slumped next to me on the tailgate. Far beyond talking, he raises his beer bottle in a vague toast.

Around us, bodies circle as wildly and erratically as the

sparks. Bass is thumping from another pickup. The whole world smells of smoke and beer. People are talking about nothing, loudly. When I let their voices blend, it seems as if they're speaking another language, one that I can't understand.

If I were sitting on the back of my own truck, I could go home right now. Maybe take the other guy with me, as an act of human kindness, and roll him out of the cab into his front yard.

But I came in Hannah's mom's Saturn. It was the only way to avoid meeting Hannah's parents. She wanted me to stop by and hang out for a while before the party.

"My dad needs the truck," I said.

Of course, then I had to explain why the truck was in the driveway when she picked me up. I don't think Hannah believed my story about his sudden-onset sinus infection. I should have just told her that he was piss-ass drunk.

She's near the fire now, glowing and giggling, greeting people as if she hasn't seen them in years—even though she probably saw them downtown this afternoon.

I've given up trying to convince her to leave. She's already called me an old man and told me to go have a drink and stop being so curmudgeonly. That was her word. "Curmudgeonly." As I stare into the fire, the sparks start to look like code. They're probably telling me to blow this party and go home to bed.

A shrill voice pierces the blur, draws my attention.

". . . and you stand here looking like the queen of Sheena. You think you can just grab a guy like an extra handful of candy from the bulk food aisle?"

I recognize Lex's voice, but I can't find her in the crowd bobbing around the fire. Beside me, the plaid-jacket guy has managed to raise his head. "Interesting comparison," he mutters. "Think she meant queen of Sheba, though." He goes back to rocking to his own internal beat, not quite in sync with the stereo bass.

"So. Completely. Unfair." Lex is shrieking now, and I finally find her silhouette near the flames. With each word, she gives her target a shove. It's Hannah. I realize belatedly that her target is *Hannah*.

"Catfight!" someone hollers.

I'm halfway off the tailgate when my companion throws an arm across my path.

"Never, ever interfere in a girl fight," he tells me, his eyes suddenly wide, boring into mine as if he's imparting some cosmic piece of understanding.

It's too late anyway. Someone else hugs Lex from behind, pinning her arms. Hannah spins and stalks away, away from Lex and away from my tailgate and into the crowd, where I see Greg step forward and Dallas throw a consoling arm around her shoulders.

Those two are good guys. Always around, always wearing the same easygoing smiles. If one of their friends decided to build himself a grizzly-proof suit, they would be there, every weekend, strapping on his armor and passing him his beer.

Hannah probably wishes I were more like them.

I watch her until she's pasted her smile back on and accepted another drink, which takes all of three minutes. And probably means I'm driving her Saturn home tonight.

I've been sitting on this tailgate for a long time.

"Going for a walk. See you later, bud."

My companion doesn't even raise his beer this time. His eyes have turned back into slits and his mouth is slack.

I sort of envy him.

I suppose what I should do is check on Hannah, make sure she's okay. That's what a good boyfriend would do. Hannah and I aren't officially boyfriend and girlfriend, though, and that has to have some benefits. Right? Benefits such as not having to meet her parents. Let Greg and Dallas take care of her. Besides, there's the cosmic wisdom to consider.

Turning away from the fire, I head down the dirt road—the one leading back toward town. The early September air feels suddenly crisp, prickling my lungs. As I walk, my eyes slowly adjust to the darkness. The woods separate themselves into individual tree trunks and the road appears as a faint gray strip in front of me. After a while, I see a flash of orange, like an ember, glowing at the side of the road.

"Is that Cole over there?"

I stop.

"Cole Owens? The one with Academy Awards in his future?"

Lauren's words float like a string of silvery bubbles in the dark. The smell of pot wafts after them.

I peer in the direction of her voice. She's facing the road, perched halfway down the slope of the ditch, her arms wrapped around her knees, a joint dangling from her fingers. "Are you sitting down there by yourself?"

"Like an island," she says.

I look from her to the gravel road. I can't walk all the way home. I definitely don't want to go back to the party yet. It's been three months. Lauren must be over our breakup by now, no matter what Lex was hollering about. It would be a relief to talk to someone normal.

"Can I join you?"

She shrugs. "Free country."

I take a running step to cross the swamp water at the bottom of the ditch. Once I'm settled, I turn to look at her more closely. This isn't the usual Lauren.

"Why are you staring at me like that?" she asks.

"It's a bit weird."

"What is?"

"You sitting here by yourself, smoking pot."

"I'm having a sit-in-the-ditch night," she says, flicking a lighter and taking a long drag as if to prove herself.

"You don't smoke."

"I do now. It's relaxing."

"Where are your friends?"

"Who knows?" she says, with a smirk that should belong to someone else. Someone more sardonic. Me, for example.

"Lex was causing a bit of a scene at the party back there."

Lauren sighs. For a few minutes, she tries unsuccessfully to blow a smoke ring. "She's overprotective these days. Why does she think it's her job to look after me?"

I have no answer for that. Taking Lauren's joint from her lips, I attempt my own smoke ring. I'm a spectacular failure. They can probably hear me hacking from the next town over.

When I can breathe again, we listen to some guys shouting from the party, followed by a loud, rolling laugh that seems to bounce over us and down the road.

For a while, I fool around with my camera's night vision and Lauren tries to blow smoke rings on film. When a frog croaks from beneath our feet, we both jump and I almost send the camera flying into the mud. It croaks a second time, as if claiming the ditch for itself. Lauren was never a fan of slimy things, but she makes no move to leave.

"You're going to get dirty sitting here," I say. I can already

130   TANYA LLOYD KYI

feel dampness soaking through the seat of my jeans. "Your butt will be wet."

"Don't care," she says.

I squint at her. "Who are you, exactly, and what have you done with the real Lauren?" The Lauren I knew would need a gun at her head before she agreed to sit in the mud, let alone smoke pot.

"This is me. With a little extra thrown in." She turns and puts a hand on my arm. "The real Lauren has changed," she whispers. "Changing every day."

She seems to think this is hysterically funny. I have to put an arm across her to keep her from sliding into the water. She wraps a hand around my arm and leans her head on my shoulder. Then, just for a second, I feel it: warmth, like one of those bonfire embers. It's not the spark of chemistry. It's more the familiar pressure of her skin and the comfort of knowing exactly where I am.

I let my cheek rest against the top of her head. Lauren and I could actually be friends. I could list her in the rolling credits one day. Maybe get her tickets to a red-carpet event. If she could get away from her husband and four kids for the weekend.

Maybe she's thinking the same things because neither of us moves.

Eventually, she says, "You know, Cole, life is about choices." She punctuates her words with conductor-like waves of the joint.

"That's deep."

She ignores my sarcasm. "Today, I had two choices. It was the very last day I had two choices. And you know what I did?"

"What?"

"Nothing. Absolutely nothing."

Apparently, I'm not good at ditch-sitting conversations. I have no idea what we're talking about. "So . . . tomorrow?"

"Nope. Tomorrow's too late. I didn't choose today, so now there's only one choice."

"One choice," I repeat. "And that is . . . ?"

"That is . . ." Lauren pauses. "Entirely my choice to make."

This seems to be the end of the topic and I have to say, I'm a bit relieved. I'm not sure I could handle any more girl logic right now. Sometimes it's better just to sit. And touch shoulders. And breathe the night air with its trace of campfire smoke and be content to stay where you are. Even if that does happen to be in a ditch.

"I miss you," she whispers after a while. Thankfully, it doesn't feel like a demand, the way it did in her living room a few weeks ago. It doesn't feel like an invitation or a complaint either. Just a statement. A simple statement.

"Me too," I say.

"It wouldn't have worked, would it?" she says.

I shake my head.

I suppose I should move. Leaning against my ex-girlfriend in the dark is not a step toward separating myself or building my new, independent life. It's comfortable here, though. I stay, feeling the warmth of her arm against mine in the cooling air, until a car rounds the bend from the gravel pit and its headlights blind me.

Lauren sits up.

"Thanks," she says, squaring her shoulders. She pats her hair. The headlights sweep across our bodies like prison yard searchlights, then the tires crunch to a stop on the gravel. Blinking the spots from my eyes and reclaiming my arm, I peer at the window. It's Greg.

"What are you guys doing out here?" he asks. He's looking only at Lauren. "Why are you in a ditch?"

So I'm not the only one who thought that was strange.

"We're . . . meditating," she says.

He gives her a lopsided smile. "When a night has gotten that far, it's usually time to head home. You want a ride?"

She turns to me, and I shrug. What am I going to do? Invite her to continue sharing her ditch with me? Offer her a ride in Hannah's mom's Saturn?

"All right," she says to Greg. "Very gentlemanly of you."

"Hey—I was gentlemanly. Didn't I just save you from sliding into the mud a minute ago?"

She looks at me as if I've just mentioned her underwear in public. Standing, pausing to brush the dirt off her ass like the real Lauren would, she steps across the ditch and onto the road with only a mild waver.

"You're very sweet. Thank you," she coos at Greg. Then she closes the car door and the wheels spin on the gravel and they're gone. Leaving me alone in the ditch.

Which may be where I belong. By myself in the dark, responsible for no one, with nobody expecting anything from me. As I ponder whether this ditch is my ideal habitat, another car rounds the corner. I stand when I recognize the Saturn. It skids to a stop just ahead of me, the window rolls down, and Hannah leans from the passenger seat.

"Cole! Climb in—we're going to Dallas's!"

Which is the last thing I want to do, but there are only so many routes out of a ditch near a gravel pit in the middle of the night. I end up squished beside Dallas and two giggling girls in the backseat.

Halfway to Dallas's house, one of the girls pukes.

I must have done something very wrong in a past life.

chapter 14

betrayal and other high school classes

A couple weeks into the new school year, I have another counselor's appointment. Everyone gets one, just like every kindergartener gets a measles vaccine. I guess they're trying to inoculate us against our own stupidity.

I'm the lucky guy with his appointment booked just as people are switching classes, giving them plenty of time to gawk at me through the glass. Squirming a little, I remember what happened with Ms. Gladwell at our botched appointment last spring. The fall. The accidental embrace. Then Dallas walks by, pumping his fist at me. I turn purple.

"Did you research the film school?" Ms. Gladwell asks when

she emerges from the inner office. "And are you okay? You look flushed."

I ignore that last part.

"I downloaded the application info. I'm supposed to submit a short film by January," I tell her as she motions me inside.

It's time to get serious about this short. And I'm all fired up by a book I found about a Scottish guy named John Grierson. He wasn't from a big city, and he wasn't rich. He was smart as hell, though.

This is what Grierson did: met Robert Flaherty (the *Nanook of the North* filmmaker) in Hollywood; invented the word "documentary"; went home to Scotland and started a movement in support of documentary film; got invited to Canada to create a report on filmmaking; became head of Canada's new National Film Board; made all the Canadian news movies about World War II, controlling what tons of people thought about the war; built one of the biggest film studios in the entire world.

The whole time I've been reading his story, I've been trying to decide whether it's hopeful. Take one: Yes, his story's inspiring. We were both born to normal families in small towns, and so there's hope that I might eventually escape Webster and create a monumental film studio, help invent a genre, and/or possibly change the trajectory of all filmmaking.

Take two: Everything's already been done, Grierson was *way* more brilliant than I can ever hope to be, and I was born in the wrong era.

"A short film. Quite an undertaking," Ms. Gladwell says. "What's your approach?"

I don't feel like explaining my Webster-as-web idea. It won't sound right, and she'll give suggestions, and I'll want to trash the entire thing.

Ms. Gladwell takes my silence to mean I need "guidance."

"Let's brainstorm a little, Cole," she says.

Or we could slice ourselves with razors. "That's okay. I'm working on some ideas. And I'm going to be late for class . . ."

"I'll write you a note," she says.

Great. Perfect. *Please excuse Cole's tardiness. He was confronting deep-seated emotional issues in the counselor's office.*

"Come on. Toss out some ideas," Ms. Gladwell prods. When did she get so forceful? I peer at her. She looks different. More . . . rosy.

"Did you get your hair cut or something?"

"Nope." She pushes a piece of paper toward me.

"If you're not ready to work on actual ideas, why don't we talk about the reasons you want to go to film school? Write a list. It doesn't have to make sense or look perfect. Just jot down whatever comes to mind."

Why would anyone want to make docs? Unless you're

Michael Moore, it doesn't get you famous. Or rich. Just look at John Grierson. After building one of the world's largest film studios for the Canadian government, he got hauled in front of a tribunal because one of his secretaries turned out to have Russian spy connections. People accused Grierson of being a communist. Which was bad, in those days. Really bad.

I must look doubtful.

"Anything you want," Ms. Gladwell says. "It can even be private. I won't look." She turns toward her bookshelf and starts flipping through a text.

I pick up the pen. I draw a spaceship shooting at alien invaders.

Okay. A list. I may as well get it over with.

Leave Webster
Make money
Work with cool people
Escape Dad, girlfriend, paella
Give autographs
Meet hot chicks

She did say it was private. I glance over my notes, then up at Ms. Gladwell, who's pretending to be absorbed in the *Diagnostic and Statistical Manual of Mental Disorders*.

I go back to my list. It's not going to cut it. Most of it's not even true.

I try again.

I think of why I love watching docs. Why my dad and I can spend an entire Saturday night watching the History Channel.

Show things in unexpected ways.
Show people things they wouldn't otherwise see.
Go behind appearances, to expose the truth.

Even a subject as ridiculous as a bear-proof suit can make you see things in a new way. I mean, Dad was right. That grizzly-obsessed guy was an idiot. But he was so passionate about his project that his friends tromped around in the mountains helping him test his ideas. And then he inspired another guy to pick up a camera and film the whole thing. Somewhere, in the footage of a guy flailing around in body armor, trying to achieve an unreasonable dream, there's a universal truth to be found.

"Let's see what you've got," Ms. Gladwell says.

"Hey! You said it would be private." This when she's already snatched the paper out of my hands.

"I lied," she says. There's definitely something different about her.

"Well, I wouldn't go with the hot chicks angle in your application letter," she says.

"It was a joke."

"I think this is what you need," she says, circling an entry. "Expose the truth. Are there filmmakers doing that now? People you admire?"

"Yeah. Some." Expose the truth. It sounds so pretentious when she says it out loud. And yet . . . When I talked about Uganda, I wonder if Lauren and Greg would have understood better if I'd used those words instead.

"Well, even in Webster, things are often more complicated than they seem," Ms. Gladwell says. "Everyone has a unique story."

"That's sort of what I was thinking." Or is it? My short is going to show the similarities in their stories, not the uniqueness. I'm exploring the ways in which they're all equally stuck.

Ms. Gladwell writes me a note on the distinctive pink counseling office paper. My deep thoughts about a meaningful film career go fluttering away as she hands it to me.

I can already hear Dallas as I pass the paper to the math teacher. "Hey, Owens, ya pregnant? Anorexic?"

I take the note reluctantly. "Thanks, Ms. Gladwell. You've been a big help."

She looks tremendously pleased with herself.

• • •

After Canada gave him the shaft, Grierson went back to Europe and worked on films for a decade or so. As I sit with Greg in the school lobby during lunch hour, filming the general chaos around me, I'm thinking Europe might be a good destination. I should move to Paris. Or Munich. Rome.

Greg has chosen a spot on the long bench by the trophy case, halfway between the main office and the student council's snack stand. Other than the glass case, the entire lobby is covered in orange terra-cotta tile. It must have been in style when they built the school, but now it looks like the basketball team ate barbecue chips, then threw up on the walls and the floor.

That's what Greg's lunch looks like too. Now that his dad's moved out, his mom's gone vegan. Which means that he's unwrapping a sandwich stuffed with alfalfa sprouts and chickpea paste. I pull out last night's leftover pizza and pass him a slice.

We're here because rain is pissing down outside as if it might never stop. It seems like half the school is milling around. For a while, I pan in on the drama students practicing some sort of lip sync at the bottom of the staircase. Then I film the point guard of the basketball team as he attempts a backward standing jump directly onto the counter of the snack stand. When he succeeds, there's a gaggle of cheering fans around him as if he just made the NBA.

I focus the camera on the counter, wondering if I could jump it. Maybe. But I don't understand why you would *want* to. I'm getting that feeling again—like the entire world's gone a little bit crazy or like everyone's speaking a dialect I don't understand. I wonder if that's part of filming, part of being a detached observer instead of a participant.

When I pan across the lobby again, my lens finds a cluster of eighth-grade girls down the bench from us, giggling their way closer. I turn off the camera so it doesn't encourage them. In my current mood, I'm likely to say something biting about their general inanity, and they'll look at me with injured eyes, and I'll feel horribly guilty for the rest of the afternoon.

Maybe I wasn't designed to be a participant.

"I think they're after you," I tell Greg.

He doesn't even glance their way. "Does Lauren look okay to you?"

I look over to where Lauren, Lex, and a few other girls are knotted together in a corner, whispering.

"She was fine the other night. A bit weird, maybe."

"She looks tired."

With a sigh, I look again. I already know what I'll see— Lauren'll be wearing yoga pants and one of her dad's old sweatshirts. Her hair will be pulled into a ponytail. She's stopped taking care of herself lately, as if she's depressed. I can't help worrying that it's my fault.

But what am I supposed to do about it? The cloud of guilt hovering over me seems unfair.

"Maybe she has a thyroid problem," I tell Greg.

"You're an insensitive bastard sometimes, you know?" Greg shakes his head.

I thought that maybe, after our sit-in-a-ditch night, things with Lauren would improve. No signs of that, though. She still ignores me, streaming around me in the school hallways as if she's water and I'm a rock.

Greg is still staring, first at her, then at me. My guilt grows.

"Since when are you so concerned about Lauren?"

Silence.

"I'm serious. What's up?"

"I just want to make sure she's okay," he says finally. "You don't need to be an asshole about it."

"Well, go ask her."

"I did," he says. He stands and peers at Lauren again, like he's considering crossing the lobby. Instead, he scuffs one toe against the floor as if he's five years old.

"What'd she say?"

"She said she's fine."

"Great." Then we can change the topic before I start banging my head against the bench in an attempt to fix things that can't be fixed. Like my brain.

"I don't think it's true," Greg says.

"You're kinda scaring me, bud."

Greg lowers himself onto the bench again. He puts his elbows on his knees and laces his fingers together, like a lawyer about to make his case. He's looking at his feet, though. And I'm staring at him like he may have been abducted and replaced by a Greg imposter.

"I think I want to ask Lauren out."

"Like on a date?"

"Yeah."

He turns to face me and I suddenly realize this is big. This is something he's been waiting to tell me for a while. This is an official announcement.

chapter 15

objects in the mirror are less real than they appear

Greg has obviously been thinking hard about the Lauren issue, looking for the right moment to tell me.

"So ask her out," I say, shrugging, glancing away in case my face looks like I just got sucker punched. I accidentally make eye contact with one of the giggling girls, which causes a squeal and a small commotion.

"It wouldn't bother you?" Greg sounds relieved.

"Why would it bother me?" Of course it'll bother me. I feel like my brother just asked if he could have sex with my sister. Which they may as well do with me in the room because I've known them both so long that I can imagine every minute of it. The way Greg will lay on the moves. The way Lauren will laugh with the tip of her tongue caught between her teeth.

I shudder, trying to shake away the images before they go too far.

"I think it'll bother you," Greg says.

"It's not going to bother me!" It comes out louder than I plan, and the eighth-grade girls scoot away from us. Greg raises his eyebrows.

"How long have you been thinking about this?" I ask. Briefly, I close my eyes. I wonder how long it would take me to study Zen meditation and learn universal acceptance.

Too long, probably. When I open my eyes, Greg looks uncomfortable.

"Seriously. It's no big deal." Except that Lauren's mine, even though she's not really mine. I'm with Hannah. Sort of. In an unofficial, casual kind of way.

The thought of Greg touching Lauren still bothers me. "I'm just curious. How long?"

"Sometime over the summer, I guess."

I'll bet he's lying. No wonder the guy hasn't had a girlfriend in ages. He's probably spent years lusting after mine. Not that Greg would ever act on something like that. Not in a million years. And knowing that—knowing he's done everything right and I'm the one being unreasonable here—makes my stomach clench even tighter.

In the official friendship handbook, I wonder what the allotted time is between "Point A: You Break Up" and "Point B: Friend Hooks Up." Especially after two years together. I'm pretty sure it's longer than three or four months. Maybe it should be equal to the duration of the actual relationship. Two years sounds about right. And that time should start from the afternoon of the red sundress, too, not from the breakup conversation.

Which is ridiculous. Objectively, with the part of my brain that's not longing to bang itself against the bench, I do realize how unreasonable this is. But that doesn't make me feel any less betrayed.

When Lauren and I broke up, it wasn't a screaming, name-calling, vase-throwing fight. As they say in the movies, no animals were harmed in the making of the scene.

No, we broke up the same way the ice melts off Mallard Lake every spring. One week, you're ice skating and the next week, you're smelling mud instead of snow. At first, there's open water only in the center. Then it creeps its way toward shore until all that's left of the ice is a crackling around the edges of the reeds.

Lauren and I were like that ice. We used to be so solid together that you could have jumped up and down on us and we would never have cracked. But slowly a gap appeared between us, and it grew.

When my mom passed away, Lauren tried to stay close to me. She really did. But somehow, I couldn't feel the same way about her. Maybe because I couldn't feel anything at all.

We broke up just after sunset, on Lauren's back porch. It's all Walt Disney perfect out there. A porch swing to sit on and clumps of puffy purple flowers around us. I could hear an occasional car on the road at the bottom of the hill. A siren swelled, then faded. Lauren's pocket dog was curled in her lap and the neighbor's German shepherd snuffled on the other side of the fence. He didn't bark. He was used to us being back there.

Lauren leaned her forehead against my chest and I breathed in the green apple smell of her shampoo.

"You know that I'm right," I said. "We're not the same anymore. We're not together in our heads. We're just pretending."

"It's those damn movies you've been watching," she muttered, half into my shirt. I'd been making her watch an endless stream of documentaries, and the dolphin killings in *The Cove* hadn't been a big hit. But Lauren was wrong about the sequence. We hadn't stopped talking because I was watching movies. I'd started watching more movies because then we didn't have to talk.

It wouldn't help to explain this, so I stroked her hair and said nothing.

Lauren was perfect, really. Smart. Pretty. Kind. I just couldn't be part of a perfect couple anymore. I'd spent months pretending to be okay until everyone else, including Lauren, seemed to think things really *were* normal. But every day still felt like a damn ice field that I had to pick my way across without falling into a crevasse.

I needed to stop trying so hard.

After a few minutes of quiet, Lauren asked, "Who am I going to hang out with?"

She sounded so sad, I wished I could take everything back. I wished I were strong enough to keep pretending, forever. "We can still hang out."

"It won't be the same."

I held her for a little while as she cried, then her mom started doing dishes—loudly—on the other side of the kitchen window. Lauren's mom is one of those tightly wound types, skinny from constantly worrying about whether she's planted the tomatoes too early or whether half an hour is too long for a sixteen-year-old to sit on the deck alone with her boyfriend.

Her ex-boyfriend.

I slowly extracted myself. Stood. Then, just for a moment, I swayed. The reality of not having Lauren to call, not having Lauren to lean on, hit me like an avalanche and I turned back to her. She had her eyes closed tight and her pointer fingers pressed to the bridge of her nose. It made my own throat close up. I almost fell, onto the swing and into her arms.

This was its own kind of death. I was killing something between us.

Lauren wants to have kids. Tons of kids. And she wants to be a stay-at-home mom until they're all in school so she can take them to the park and bake chocolate chip cookies and all those other things she thinks good moms do. After dating for two years, you know certain things. And I knew, as I stepped away from that porch swing, that she was thinking about her imaginary herd of kids and how they might not have my shoulders, or my chin, anymore.

Families don't always turn out like you plan. Sometimes they fall apart when you're not the least bit ready.

I kissed Lauren on the cheek, then I took a deep breath and held it as I walked away, leaving her on the swing, arms wrapped tightly around herself. I made it all the way back to my truck before I cried.

In the school foyer, one of the younger girls has finally minced her way in front of us.

"I just wanted to s-say . . . she likes you," she stutters.

I can't tell whether she's talking to me or to Greg, and I have no idea which one of her gaggle of friends is "she." Both Greg and I ignore her until she skitters away.

"Lauren and I broke up months ago," I tell Greg. "If you want to ask her out, talk to her, not me."

"Yeah . . . maybe," Greg says, as if it doesn't matter one way or the other. Which is irritating because if he's going to talk to her, I'd at least like to know when. That way I can turn on strobe lights and blast some music so I don't have to imagine seeing or hearing them together.

When the girls start giggling again, I get off the bench.

"I have to get out of here for a while," I say. "Screw the rain."

But it's torrential. It's *Inconvenient Truth*, climate-change-level rain, and there's really no way to disregard it. I end up huddled against the doorway, staring at the parking lot and feeling like crap.

When Friday night finally rolls around, I'm driving with Hannah, and the only thought in my head is this: Lauren is out with Greg. Right at this very moment. Probably also driving somewhere. Somewhere in the shadows, maybe up a steep gravel road like this one, lit only by headlights, curtains of evergreens leaning in from either side.

"We should name this truck," Hannah says. As if sensing my discomfort, she's put on her best and brightest bimbo act.

"Guys don't name trucks. That's a girl thing."

"I'm thinking Hank. Hank's a good name."

"Hank." The trouble with women is their need to have conversations about nothing. In all those girl magazines—the ones that apparently teach them how to put on eye makeup and how to get guys to call them back "the day after"—they should have articles about how not to talk about nothing.

"Save Your Relationship: Speak Substance"
"Trade Your Flapping for Focus"
"Take Back the Yap"

"Hank is a good name," Hannah says again. "It has that forestry dude personality. Hank. The truck of love." She reaches across the console and playfully traces a finger up my thigh.

What if Lauren is naming Greg's car right now?

I think the problem is this: There are only three people I like to hang out with. Greg, Lauren, and Hannah. Despite the pressure of her fingers on my thigh, I am doing my best to keep Hannah at arm's length. So if Greg and Lauren become a unit, together, separate from me . . .

But that's what I want, right? Distance. No attachments, no strings. Freedom to be my own man, make my own decisions, and leave town at the end of the school year. It's what I want.

I hit the gas, sending gravel spraying from beneath the tires. We take the next corner a little too fast.

We're on our way up Goat Mountain, which is almost directly behind my house. Somewhere up here is the hang-glider takeoff, a wooden platform that seems to jut from the cliff into the sky.

Hannah's fingers are sliding high on my leg, exploring.

I see the pullout, finally, and swing the truck off the road. As soon as I cut the engine, darkness floods in like water. The silhouettes of the trees are barely visible on either side of us, and they drop away into nothingness just ahead. Above, the stars are so clear they seem artificial, like an on-set re-creation of a perfect sky.

My fly is unzipped. Somehow Hannah reaches all the way across me and over the side of the seat to hit the recline button, tilting me backward.

"Very acrobatic."

She tugs gently at my waistband, kissing the skin beneath. I can feel the blood draining from my limbs and pouring into my crotch.

"Isn't it strange that no one in the world knows where we are?" she murmurs.

I make a strangled sound of agreement.

"And there are other people in dark spots all over these mountains, and no one knows where they are, but you can feel them. It's like we're all connected."

Why did she have to say that?

All the stirrings she's roused disappear and I deflate like a punctured balloon. I'm limp just in time for her palm to rest on my crotch.

I feel her pause. She doesn't stop immediately. She nibbles all the way up to my neck.

"What are you thinking about, Cole?" she whispers.

What am I supposed to tell her? Oh, I'm just imagining my ex-girlfriend going down on my best friend and their heartbeats joining with our heartbeats in some great cosmic fuckup.

"I'm just—I'm just in a strange mood," I say. "Sorry. I should have stayed home."

"That's okay," she says. "We can sit and talk for a while. It's always gorgeous here."

Always?

"I guess you've been here before."

She smirks. "And you haven't?"

"I like the stars," I counter.

"Do you know the constellations? I've always wanted to learn them." She's sincere, willing to brush off my grumpiness and impotence and look at star patterns. Like Orion and his giant sword. Which is probably what Lauren's looking at right now. A giant, phallic . . .

"Let's get out of here," I say, raising my seat back and reaching for the ignition.

"No. Wait. We just got here. We can talk about stuff."

"Like what?" Inwardly, I groan. I want to go home, press a pillow over my head, and wait for daylight. But of course she wants to talk. She's a girl.

"Well, I've been wanting to talk about Vancouver."

"What about it?" I really have to publish that magazine article, "The Undiscovered Relationship Secret: Silence."

"You're going to be there next year. And if I go to UBC, I'll be nearby."

Too late for a graceful escape, I understand where this is going.

"My mom and dad took me to Vancouver last summer, to see the school," she says.

"Really?" Maybe she wants to describe the campus. I hold on to that hope.

And I wonder if my mom would have taken me, shown me her favorite spots when she was a student. She would have at least asked what I was planning. Dad's never even asked.

"UBC's out on a point, at the very west edge of Vancouver.

It's not too far from downtown, where you'll be if you go to the film school. About twenty minutes away."

She just mentioned us in relation to each other in Vancouver.

"Hey, can you believe how clear it is out there?" In a fairly desperate attempt to change the subject, I lean forward to peer out the windshield. But then I accidentally focus on Orion, which makes me think of Greg and Lauren again. Orion is the only constellation I know, other than the Dippers. His stupid sword sticks out of the sky as if it's made of neon.

"You'll have roommates, I guess," Hannah says. "But if I'm in residence, I'll probably have my own dorm room."

I sigh. She's not going to be distracted by stars. Which means there's only one way out of this conversation.

"Did anyone ever tell you that girls talk too much?" This time, I lean toward her, and I have to say, I'm impressively acrobatic myself.

After a while, I brush her hair out of the way and whisper in her ear. "Go back to what you were doing before."

And she does.

chapter 16

and the parenting award of the year goes to . . .

I catch Dallas outside the bank on Sunday afternoon. He looks as if he just rolled out of bed and his initial response to being filmed isn't too positive.

"I'll owe you one. Or a case," I tell him, and he reluctantly agrees.

"Okay. First question. Are you going to stick around next year, or are you heading back to Dallas?"

He runs a hand through his bedhead hair. "Did I ever tell you exactly what went down in Texas?"

"Nope." Maybe catching people half-asleep is good. Maybe they're more vulnerable, more willing to spill private information.

"Yeah, well, my mom took off, and not just with anybody—with the minister."

My hands tighten on the camera. This could be perfect for the short. It could imply that Webster isn't the only trap. The suffocation of life in a small town is universal, and people will do unexpected things to escape. Forcing myself to breathe slowly, to keep the camera absolutely steady, I try to think what to ask next. How do I get more out of him? But Dallas continues on his own.

"You know, I'm not actually from Dallas, despite the nickname y'all gave me. We lived in this oil town in the middle of nowhere. A bunch of guys making cash on the rigs, then blowing it in the bars. That town was one big party."

It sounds like Dallas's ideal habitat. "So you're not going back, or you are?"

"Nah. My dad and my brother are here. I'll try to get a job around here too. It's kinda peaceful, you know?"

"It's peaceful? Your house is always full of people. It's a zoo."

"Really?" he asks, considering.

"Um, yeah." No house has ever been less peaceful.

"Nah, it's friends. Hanging out, you know? I like to have people around. That's part of why I like it here. There's good people."

When did this interview go off the rails? We were doing so

well with the adultery and desertion references, and now we're talking warm and fuzzy.

"So, you're going to stay." I've given up.

Dallas nods. "It's a nice place."

I snap the camera closed. And despite the utter uselessness of the clip, I go home and stream it into the computer. Somewhere in the interviews I've done and the scenes I've shot here and there, there must be salvageable material.

There must be. But I stare at the screen for hours without finding it.

I wake with a start, not sure if the noise was real or in my dream. My face is stuck to the keyboard. I must have fallen asleep editing. I stagger to bed.

Then, just as I'm closing my eyes, it comes again. A thunk—something hitting wood—then a scrape.

The clock reads 2:15.

Wide awake now, I get up and head for the stairs, looking for something to carry with me. The best I find is a hardcover book on my way through the rec room. *The American Film Institute Catalog of Motion Pictures, Vol. 4*. It doesn't seem as lethal as I'd like, but maybe I can bash an intruder over the head with it if necessary.

The scraping sound again. It's as if someone's trying to wedge a piece of metal into our front door, trying to pry it open.

I stop just before the top of the stairs. I can see the front door on the landing above me, and someone's definitely out there.

Our front door is like every other front door in town. White. Brass doorknob. Frosted glass panel on the top half. There's something pressed against that panel right now. Someone.

I could call my dad. I would, if he hadn't passed out after dinner. He's probably comatose.

I could call the police. Then, even if I opened the door, I'd at least have backup on the way. Of course, by the time I call anyone, the intruder might be inside the house.

Scrape. A shoulder shoves against the door with a thud.

Backup would be good.

Okay, I have a plan. I'm going to haul open the door and catch this bastard. At the same time, I'm going to yell like hell for my dad. That way, even if I'm outmatched, I only have to last minutes until it's two-on-one. Assuming Dad wakes up.

I press myself against the wall, then reach to curl my fingers around the cold metal of the doorknob, careful not to show myself in the glass. With my other hand, I raise *The American Film Institute Catalog* above my head.

One . . . two . . . deep breath . . . three . . .

"Dad! Dad!"

Hollering like a crazy man, I whip open the door so fast the intruder actually falls into the house, landing facedown in the dark, his feet still outside. I throw myself over him, straddling his waist, ready to slam the book into his skull—

"Cole?"

This is my backup. But the voice isn't coming from the living room or from Dad's bedroom. The voice is coming from the floor.

I chuck the book to the side, and it hits the closet door like a brick.

I can't even swear. That's how hard my heart is pounding.

I slide off Dad and sit on the vinyl floor of the landing, leaning my head against the wall and breathing in the smell of my own sweat. The front door's still open and the streetlight's glow seeps in along with the cold air.

"Guess I scared you, eh?" Dad says. He's managed to roll onto his back, but his chest is heaving. I must have knocked the wind out of him. "I always said you were built like a brick shit house," he wheezes.

"And just as smart." I finish the joke for him, but I'm not finding it very funny at the moment. "You almost got your block knocked off by a first-edition film catalog."

"A what?"

"That book! I almost cracked your skull open with the book!" What a headline that would be. Son knocks out father with secondhand hardcover. That book was hard to find, too. I'd hate to have wrecked it.

"That was the best you could do for a weapon?" Dad asks. "What kind of guy attacks someone with a book?"

"What kind of guy tries to break into his own house?"

For some reason, Dad finds this hilarious. And maybe it is because it's the middle of the night, but when he gasps, "My keys. I couldn't get my keys in the damned hole," he's laughing so hard that he's wiping tears from his eyes. A dog starts to bark outside.

"We should close the door," Dad says finally, catching his breath a little.

"You're *in* the door," I tell him. As he struggles to remove himself from the threshold, it becomes even more obvious why his keys weren't working. He's piss drunk.

"How did you even get out there?" I ask. "You were asleep in the living room."

"I guess I woke up." Dad drags himself to standing, staggers into the wall, rights himself, turns with the careful deliberation of a robot, and heads for his room.

"Don't worry. I'll lock up," I call after him, scowling. How am I supposed to live an independent life if my dad can't unlock his own front door? How am I supposed to leave town?

He raises one hand to wave a vague thank-you and continues toward bed.

I should have whacked him on the head after all, I think as I stumble back downstairs. Or I should have called the police for backup so they could have had a talk with him about decent parenting skills.

Now it looks like I'm in charge of having that talk.

"We can't keep going like this."

Dad eyes me warily from the kitchen table, where he's clutching a mug of coffee. The first touch of morning sun glimmers though the side window. In film terms, it's the magic hour. Dawn brightens the street, but as a car drives past, its headlights are still on. Perfect lighting for an imperfect scene.

"Going like what?" Dad asks.

"This." I try to put the whole weight of our situation into one word.

"Not getting you, Cole."

"There's no food in the fridge. The house looks like crap. You haven't shaved. And you're probably still drunk from last night. How are you going to go to work?"

"I'm fine. I just had a few with some friends at the hotel."

I give up, stomp into the living room, and collapse on the couch. This is messed up. I shouldn't be responsible for having this conversation. It's all backward. This isn't in my job description. He's supposed to be the parent, not me.

The silence grows uncomfortably long. My breath seems too loud.

"We could move, you know," I yell finally.

"What?" he calls.

"We could move. Head to the coast or somewhere new, where we don't know anyone."

"What the hell are you going on about?" When Dad comes out of the kitchen, he's looking at me as if I've grown two heads.

"I'm saying we have to change something."

He grunts. "I wouldn't worry about that. I have a feeling things are going to start changing, whether we like it or not."

What the hell is that supposed to mean? I stare at the carpet, wondering how, exactly, to fix this situation. Even if we didn't change cities, we could change houses. Move to an apartment, maybe. At some point, Dad's going to be living here by himself. Selling the house would be terrible, though. We'd have to clean out Mom's things. We'd have to clean up, and that could possibly kill us.

But something has to change.

I assume Dad is thinking about this too, until he turns away.

"I'm going to work," he proclaims. "You should get your ass to school."

Great. That went just perfectly. If filmmaking doesn't work out, I'll be sure to put drug and alcohol counselor on my list of career options.

As the door shuts behind him, I squeeze my head in my hands as if I might squish a solution from my brain. And I do, eventually, once I calm down enough to think straight. The answer is this: I'm leaving town. Whether or not my dad can keep his life together, I'm getting out.

chapter 17

male bonding: the mockumentary

Greg and I are killing zombies. He's killing most of them by himself since he gets absorbed in the game and forgets to share the controller. But that's okay. Tonight, I'm content to sit on his living room couch and provide moral support.

His date with Lauren went really badly.

This probably shouldn't make me so happy. I *want* Lauren to move on. That girl deserves everything she wants out of life. But not necessarily now. And not with Greg.

I smile, just as Greg blows the head off some dead creature with a chain-saw-massacre-style blood splatter. He takes my expression for approval. Apparently, this new gaming system was a present from his dad, probably to make up for bailing on the marriage.

"Good graphics," I say.

At least there's no sign of a stripper in his dad's life. Maybe Greg's not fully appreciating what he now has: two available parents, two bedroom choices, and a supply of guilt-driven gifts. Some would say he's got it made. He should probably stay home and enjoy it instead of chasing certain ex-girlfriends.

I find myself grinning again. Greg told me Lauren had seemed into things at first. Then they drove over the border for pizza and couldn't find anything to talk about in the car. On the way home, Lauren had some sort of food poisoning and threw up. Basically, their relationship is doomed.

"I don't think zombie blood would actually spurt," I say as he kills another batch. "Aren't they already dead? Do you think their hearts still beat?"

Greg snorts and turns up the volume.

"Watch this," he says, switching to the sniper rifle. Zooming in, he targets one across a courtyard and fires. There's the blood spurt again. And this time, a single eye pops from the zombie's head and rolls onto the cobblestones.

If there's one thing in the world that would be a turnoff for Greg, it's a girl throwing up in his car. He loves that car. In video game terms: epic fail.

"Nice shot," I say.

"I should play video games for a living." He nods.

"If we were getting paid, we'd be loaded right now. I think we've been playing for five hours."

"I'm going to be like that kid in the news who had a seizure," he says.

"Or the guy who dropped dead after forty-eight straight hours of online raiding."

"Cool," Greg says.

Then, after a minute, he hits pause and rests his head on the back of the couch. "We couldn't do this with Lauren and Hannah, you know."

"Nope."

"So who needs 'em?"

"Exactly."

The next night, as Greg and I sit at a wrought-iron table on the sidelines of the school Halloween dance, I'm thinking I should have taken his theory more seriously. We should have stayed home and played video games.

For one thing, Lex has been glaring at me all night. She's about the height of a *Wizard of Oz* munchkin, so it shouldn't be disconcerting. But it is.

"You're right, you know. Women are just as bad as everyone says," I tell Greg, yelling over the music.

"Nope," he says.

"Seriously?"

"They're worse." He scowls, crossing his arms over his chest.

Lex is pouring punch at the table along the side wall of the gym. Between filling glasses, she pauses to sneer at me again. I shake my head. Lex and I have never been close, but she's Lauren's best friend. We've spent a lot of time together, and she's never given me the evil eye before.

"Why is she doing that? Do you think she hates doctors?" I'm dressed in a lab coat because Hannah was desperate to wear a sexy nurse costume and convinced that we had to dress in coordinating outfits. Her idea, not mine. But after seeing her in her white miniskirt and those stockings . . . Well, if all I had to do was turn up at the Halloween dance with a stethoscope, that seems a small concession.

Greg is chewing on a stalk of wheat. Other than that, he's dressed in the same clothes he wears every day. According to him, he's in costume as a farmer.

He mumbles something around the wheat, but I can't hear him over the music.

"What?"

He removes the stalk. "She doesn't hate doctors," he yells. "She hates you."

I nod. "But why?"

"Can we talk about this later? I'm watching your girlfriend dance."

I shoot Greg a look. It seems a little early to be commenting about another girlfriend of mine. But the guy has such an expression of joy on his face, it's hard to take that away. Who can blame him? Hannah is gyrating against a vampire. A witch, an alien, and some sort of odd tree/clothesline combination are dancing around her.

"That girl is like a porch light attracting moths," Greg says.

"You know that kills the moths, right?"

"Who cares? You're a lucky man, Cole."

Hannah now has an alien grinding against her. Shifting out of his crotch reach, she beckons me to the dance floor. I'm considering it when something icy and wet sluices over my head and down my neck.

"What the—?" I leap to my feet, wiping my face on my arm so I can see. Lex is standing beside my chair, empty glass clutched in her fist. Her teeth are clenched and her limbs are tensed like the psycho girl in a Quentin Tarantino film.

"How can you just sit there like everything's normal?" she spits.

I open my mouth, then close it again. Isn't everything normal? This seems like a trick question.

"Do you know where Lauren is tonight? She's at home, feeling like crap."

"Okay . . ." What does she want me to do about this?

"She's a mess!" Lex says, as if I might have missed the point.

"Sorry?" I offer.

"You're not sorry." Lex has a very strange way of moving her lips more than is necessary to form her words. I've noticed it before, but it's more obvious when her face is this close to mine.

"Lex, it's more than three—no, four—months after Lauren and I broke up, and I'm supposed to know that she has the flu?"

Normally I would be mad. I do, after all, have a trail of sticky juice trickling down my back. But I'm starting to wonder if Lex is having some sort of mental break. It might be best to keep her calm.

"Lex, you know I'm not a real doctor, right? This is a costume. Cos-tume." From the corner of my eye, I see Greg crack up.

Lex throws her cup at me this time. She's only a hairsbreadth away from me and the cup is plastic. I don't think it has quite the effect she's hoping for.

"You're a bastard."

With one last glare, she turns and stalks out of the gym.

I collapse back in my chair. Greg is laughing so hard he's wiping tears from his eyes. He extracts a flask from his pocket and passes it over.

"Like I said," he yells. "You're a lucky man."

Hannah is waving me toward her again. When I shake my head, she comes to get me, hands outstretched. Her breasts . . . well, they cannot be contained by that nurse uniform.

"Come dance," she shouts.

"I can't!" I lift my arms, exposing my purple-with-punch lab coat.

"What happened?"

"An unsatisfied patient."

"Poor thing!" She leans toward me, smiling. "We'd better go. I can nurse you back to health."

It is the best offer I've had all night and I allow myself to be led from the gym.

"Lucky man," Greg calls after me. "You're a lucky man."

Which could be true, if Hannah comes home with me. And if Dad's out of the house. And if I can concentrate on this girl's nursing skills, not on the crapload of craziness in life. If all those things happen, I might possibly be a lucky man.

Dad got a load of logs delivered for firewood. I get home from a trip downtown on Sunday to find him bucking them with his chain saw.

When I see him in his work shirt, sweat stains spreading from beneath his arms, and when I smell the mix of gasoline and dusty-sweet sawdust hanging in the cold air, it's like a dose of relief is injected into my veins. I feel it traveling through me. I guess I hadn't realized how worried I've been that Dad might become permanently sunk in his recliner, remote control in one hand and beer in the other. Maybe I've been waiting for the day when he doesn't haul himself up in time for work.

I'm about to offer my help when I see the beer sitting on a stump, a few steps away.

Of course he couldn't leave his drink inside.

I stomp by him and into the house. Over the buzz of the blade cutting into the next block of fir and the chips flying like wood turned to waterfalls, I doubt he even notices I'm home.

Now I need a beer.

Upstairs, I crack open a bottle and wander to the kitchen window, where I can peer down into the driveway. Dad's got a rhythm going. The chain saw slices through as if the log's a jelly roll. Sweep, sweep, sweep and the tree lies in pieces, ready to be axed into woodstove-size chunks. Dad's done this every fall that I can remember. A couple years ago, my mom and I would have been out there with him, rolling hunks of wood out of his way and, later, stacking the chopped pieces into a neat, jigsaw-puzzle pile under the overhang of the carport.

Below me, Dad pauses to arrange a new log. He sets the chain saw on a large stump in the middle of the driveway. Then he kicks some rounds out of the way and begins to roll a new log into position.

The chain saw's still roaring.

As I watch, it vibrates its way through a slow circle, the blade getting closer and closer to the backs of Dad's legs as he struggles with the next log. He's not looking.

I glance at the stairs, calculating the amount of time it will take me to run down to the garage door, skirt past the saw, and alert Dad to the danger. Too long. The blade will be at his leg before then. I could bang on the window. But even if he hears me above the motor, he might step back into the blade when he turns.

There's no way to warn him. It's like watching a horror film when you know the murderer's lurking in the next room and the lead actor steps closer and closer. All you want to do is shout at the screen, but there's no way you can stop the lead as he puts his hand on the handle and the door creaks open. . . .

Here, there's nothing to do but stand with my breath locked in my lungs, one hand clenched around my beer bottle so tightly the glass might shatter. The saw blade rattles on its stump, creeping still nearer.

He turns. At the last possible moment, he turns. With a surprised look at the blade, Dad dances out of the way and steps around to grasp the handle. Then, without much of a pause (because, unlike me, he hasn't spent the last moments in a frozen panic) and without glancing up (because he doesn't know I was about to watch him amputate a limb on our driveway), he's bucking the next log. Slice, slice, slice, so casually it should be illegal.

I consider locking myself in my room. Next year, I'm not going to be around. If he cuts himself up, he'll bleed out before anyone notices. Part of me thinks he may as well practice his independence now. But of course, I put my half-empty beer in the sink, dig my work boots out of the closet, and head outside.

Once there, I take a deep breath. There's really nothing better than the smell of freshly cut wood and air just cold enough to remind you that you'll need the woodstove soon. If I help stack the damn wood one last time, it's not because I'm going to stick around and become Dad's safety net. It's because I happen to like the smell of sawdust.

After I roll a few sections out of the way, Dad turns off the saw. He holds it in one fist, as if it's as light as a beer, and wipes his face on his other sleeve.

"You know Sheri?" he says.

"Not as well as you do."

"Don't be a smart-ass."

This is somewhat deserved, and I remain silent as I roll another log.

"That night you picked us up on the street, that wasn't the first time I seen her."

You know, there are appropriate places for this sort of thing. In Catholic churches, for example. There are dark, carved-wood booths with heavy curtains across the front where you can confess your sins to a priest instead of your son.

"I mean, it hasn't been all that long," he says. "And I sure as hell didn't plan for this to happen, but . . ."

"Whatever, Dad. No worries. I'm going to go over to Greg's for a while." If he's going to emote about Sheri, he can buck the logs by himself and cut off his leg for all I care.

"I'm trying to tell you something here. Will you hold your horses for a damned minute?"

"You know what? I don't really want to hear it. Mom's been gone barely more than a year. A year. It's bad enough that you're screwing a stripper. Now you want to tell me your love story? I don't want to hear it." I give the log a kick, which hurts, and which also feels a little juvenile after I've done it. I suppose I can't be the mature one in this family a hundred percent of the time.

"Sheri's expecting."

"Expecting what?"

"She's pregnant."

"She's *what*?" I was worried about the chain saw, and he's dropping fucking atomic bombs.

"Sheri's pregnant," Dad says, not looking at me. He's gazing out over the street as if the answer to his problems might drive up. He's still holding the chain saw. This is good because if it were on the stump, I might be tempted to pick it up and use it as a weapon. I might make that horror film into a reality.

"She told me a few days ago," he says. "The night when—"

"She's pregnant," I repeat, interrupting. "That's great."

Dad looks momentarily hopeful.

"So, you going to raise the kid on beer? Pay for its college tuition with Sheri's stripping wages? That's great, Dad. Fucking fantastic. Where the hell is this kid going to live?"

"We haven't talked about that yet," he says. "I sorta thought Sheri might move in."

I can't hear about this anymore. The idea of Sheri's stuff taking residence in my mom's dresser drawers seems momentously obscene. Worse than Sheri having a baby. A freakin' baby! My dad's old enough to be a grandpa. What the hell kind of forty-year-old man gets a stripper pregnant?

"Let me know when you have it all figured out," I spit. I kick the log again. I can't help it. Then I take off down the hill. If I could keep going and never set foot in the house again, that would be completely fine by me.

chapter 18

useful life skills, such as origami

I've barricaded myself in the rec room downstairs, so I don't pay any attention to the doorbell until I hear her voice.

"Mr. Owens," Hannah gushes. "It's so nice to finally meet you. I'm Hannah, a friend of Cole's from school." Nice. She shows up at the front door—not the basement door, like any normal human being—and rings the bell. She may as well start selling Girl Scout cookies.

My lecherous, baby-making dad is putty in her hands. I think he's actually drooling by the time I scramble upstairs. And no wonder. She's wearing high leather boots in a style no Girl Scout has ever worn.

"Did you want to come in for lunch?" he asks Hannah. "I make a mean grilled cheese."

Or you could kill me now and save me the torture of a "family" meal.

"We're going out for lunch," I blurt.

Hannah's eyes widen, but she says nothing. Just smiles.

"You . . . have a good . . . have fun," Dad says, like a TV parent who's forgotten his next line.

I stomp out of the house, taking Hannah's hand to make sure she follows me down the stairs. Months of careful avoidance on my part and she practically ruined it by showing up at the front door and introducing herself to my dad. As "a friend from school," so I can't even legitimately be mad at her for overstepping the boundaries of our casual relationship. Next thing you know, she'll be applying to babysit the newborn.

When I glance at her from the corner of my eye, she's smiling. Why would I want to go to lunch with someone so underhanded?

This is the last time I'm getting conned, I can say that much.

Hannah pretends to be oblivious. The whole way downtown, she tells me about her dreams of dog ownership. Fortunately, before I have to hear the word "labradoodle" for the sixth or seventh time, we run into Greg outside Burger Barn. Now they can entertain each other while they stuff themselves with cheeseburgers and hot chocolates.

"How's your coffee?" Hannah smiles across the table at me.

"Bad."

She slides her mug over. "Why are you drinking it then? Share mine."

I shake my head. I need to acquire a taste for coffee. I'm pretty sure Spike Lee and Errol Morris don't drink cocoa.

Greg takes a long slurp. "Delicious."

I glare at him.

He finishes his burger with a loud belch and apologizes to Hannah. Then he leans back in the booth, arms behind his head, eyes scanning the street.

There's an insider hierarchy to Burger Barn seating. The red booths run parallel to Canyon Street. If you sit with your back to the street, like I am, you have a view of the pimpled tenth-grade kids who work flipping burgers. It's not too exciting. If you sit facing the street, as Greg and Hannah have chosen to do, you see everything. You see who's bought a new car, what new couple is driving around together, or what ninth-grade kid is dying of embarrassment while his mother holds his hand on the sidewalk.

Greg loves to sit facing the street. And to tell you the truth, it doesn't matter to me. Whatever's going on out there is an encore of what went on the week before and the year before that and probably the whole generation before that. It only *seems* different, temporarily.

Besides, I can read the news off their faces. Right now, without turning, I can tell by the constant honking and Hannah's sappy expression that there's a procession of wedding cars cruising by, probably festooned with plastic pink and white flowers. Yup, there's the rattle of the tin cans.

"Do you guys want to get married and have kids?" Hannah asks.

I suck in a breath through my teeth. I should tell them. Tell them about Dad and Sheri, the baby. I should warn them, because who knows when the woman is going to turn up in our house with a watermelon belly?

Instead of answering Hannah's question, Greg blurts, "My dad wants my sister and me to move into the apartment with him."

Hannah and I both gape. Here I'm trying to ease into my shocking news and Greg flings his on the grill like a Burger Barn double patty.

"When? When did he say that?" I ask.

But we all get distracted before he can answer. A couple of nutcases are screaming at each other as they pull their crew cab into the parking lot. They're so loud, even I turn around to look.

"You want to do this right now?" A dark-haired woman is hollering, leaping down from the truck. "Right now?"

The sound carries through the windows and cinder-block walls.

I don't recognize the couple. Maybe they're tourists, passing through. Though they don't look like typical vacationers. They're both tall and skinny—too skinny—with that slouched-shoulder posture that says they don't spend their time drinking green tea and eating whole grains. They drag two little kids out of the backseat and they pull them into the restaurant, plunk them in a booth, and shove a drink in front of each. Then they head out the door.

When I turn back to the table, Hannah's wince and Greg's scowl have reached new extremes.

"Dad asked us a couple nights ago," Greg says. "My sister and I are supposed to decide for ourselves."

"That's crazy!" Hannah protests. "How are you supposed to decide that?"

"Yeah. My sister said right away she was staying with Mom, but I don't know. . . ."

I feel a surge of anger on Greg's behalf. Maybe I'm feeling a little sensitive to bad parenting at the moment or maybe I just understand how unfair it feels. You think you're living a normal life, then suddenly your world gets tipped by something out of your control. It *is* unfair. One more year and Greg would have been getting his own place. One more year and I'd have been gone and I never would have had to face my house the way it is right now.

The tourist couple is screaming at each other again. Screaming. Right in the parking lot. As if the inside of Burger Barn is soundproof and their kids and the rest of us won't hear.

"She thinks she can just walk into my house and organize everything, fuckin' take over," the woman yells.

"If you weren't passed out on the damn couch, she wouldn't have to take over."

"You were supposed to wake me up!"

"Now there's a happy marriage for you," I say.

"Those poor kids," Hannah whispers.

My eyes slide toward them—a boy and a girl, both too young for school. They're drinking their milk shakes without talking, without glancing out the window or looking around. The smaller one—maybe three or four years old—is kicking his feet against the table leg in a low, constant drum.

"As least their parents got them milk shakes," Greg says.

"I don't think that counts as good decision making," Hannah replies.

Greg is obsessively folding and refolding our napkins, as if he belongs in a loony bin. I can hardly blame him. I'd like to go outside and shut those people up.

"What are you going to do?" I say, trying to focus on the problems at my own table.

Greg's gaze flicks toward the kids.

"I mean about your dad," I clarify.

His cheeks puff as he blows a long breath. "What if he has a girlfriend? Do you think that's why he moved out? If I go with him, my mom will freak out and I'll be living with my dad and some—"

"Stripper," I finish. I know we're both picturing a bleached-blond woman staggering down Canyon Street with my dad.

Hannah looks mildly confused, but I don't bother to explain. If she doesn't already know what Sheri does for a living, she can ask around town and get the whole story.

"Would you move in with your dad, assuming there wasn't a stripper?" I ask.

What about when my dad moves in with his stripper? The idea's like a medicine ball to my gut. I start to freak out even thinking about it.

"Maybe." The way Greg is scowling, no one would want to live with him. His eyebrows drawn together and his teeth clenched, he looks like Cro-Magnon man. He should live in a cave somewhere.

Outside, the woman puts both hands on the guy's shoulders and shoves. She must be stronger than she looks because he hits the window with a vibrating thud. Every customer in the place stares except the kids. Those two gaze resolutely at the tabletop.

With more yelling, the guy shoves her back.

"This is ridiculous." I slam down my coffee cup and stand up. Maybe I can't do anything about Sheri or Greg's dad, but I can definitely put a stop to this situation.

Hannah, with stunt-girl dexterity, scrambles over the back of the booth and leaps between me and the door.

"Cole, what are you doing?" she says.

I glance over my shoulder. Greg is standing behind me, as I knew he would be. He's still holding his napkins, though, which is a bit weird.

"Hannah, get out of the way."

"You're going to end up in a fight. And fighting those two, in front of their kids, is not going to fix things," she says. She's sort of whispering, as if that will keep the kids from hearing. Fat chance.

"Is this what you want them to see?" she asks. "You and Greg beating the crap out of their dad?"

Okay, she has a point. But at least she acknowledges that we *could* beat the crap out of him.

"What are we supposed to do, then?" I'm still flexing my fists, not completely ready to let go of the idea. It would feel good to hit someone.

"Let's just go," Greg says. He turns toward the other exit.

As we walk past the kids' booth, Greg slides something onto their table. I glance down to see that he's folded his napkins into two paper hats and two paper boats. The boats have five bucks each tucked into them.

This is unexpected.

The kids stare at their prizes, openmouthed.

Looking from Greg to the paper boats and back again, I find my feet have stopped moving. I have to jog a couple steps to follow Hannah and Greg out the door farthest away from the screamers.

I wish I'd made those boats.

"You're a good guy, Greg," I tell him, once we're finally out of the splatter zone.

"Whatever," he says.

"I'm serious. That was cool. And who knew you were so skilled with origami?"

"Shut up."

It's good advice. I'm pumped up to fight, and the unused adrenaline's addling me. If I'm not careful, I'm going to end up scrapping with Greg on somebody's lawn the way we would have when we were six.

Meanwhile, Hannah's still in counseling mode. "You have to ask your dad exactly what his plans are, Greg," she says. "Just ask him."

Greg nods solemnly, like he's the psychologist's guest on a daytime TV show.

I can't help grunting. Hannah seems to think that everything can be solved through judicious use of communication skills. Why can't she just admit that some things are permanently fucked up?

"My dad's girlfriend is pregnant," I blurt. If Greg can announce game changers, so can I.

"Seriously?" Hannah squeals. "That's so exciting! When is she due?"

I shudder. I didn't even ask when Sheri was due. For all I know, she's popping out a baby right this second.

Greg's jaw drops. "Whoa. That has to freak you out a little."

"Of course it's freaking me out! My dad is having a baby with a stripper. Which part of that should I *not* freak out about?" I feel like they're not taking this seriously.

After a few steps, Greg says, "It's a bit weird, isn't it? Not so long since your mom . . ."

Now Hannah looks sympathetic, which really isn't better.

"That's tough," she says, shaking her head.

There's a moment's pause, and I wait for them to tell me how to resolve this situation. For example, they might advise me to move out—immediately. Or to demand that my dad rent Sheri a separate apartment.

"They've got me trapped," he says on the way back up the hill. "The whole 'rock and a hard place' thing."

"Buddy, you were trapped the minute you were born. This whole place is a pit, and we're stuck in it," I say.

"Thanks," he mutters. "That's encouraging."

"Hey, if your best friend won't tell you the truth, who will?"

"I still think you're trying to make decisions without enough information," Hannah insists. The girl is annoyingly reasonable.

"Sounds about right," Greg agrees.

"Tell them you need time," she says. "Hang out for a while and see what happens."

This could apply to my relationship with Hannah, now that I think about it.

Things could be worse. And soon, I'll be out of this town altogether.

As for Greg . . . well, maybe it's time for him to get out too. "You should sign up for some courses in Vancouver after grad," I say. "We could be roommates. Cool apartment, great nightlife . . ."

He grunts.

"You and me in the big city . . . ," I say.

"Focusing on the present," Hannah persists, "tell them that this has taken you by surprise. Ask them to give you a month to think about it."

"It must have been hard on your dad too," Greg says finally.

"Some people don't know how to be alone," Hannah agrees.

"At least this way, once you head to Vancouver, he'll have family around."

Worst. Friends. Ever.

Now they're yammering about decision-making processes and the differences between the ways that men and women make choices. *What the hell?*

I flip my hood over my head so their voices are muffled. My life has turned into a Woody Allen film stocked with emotionally inept characters.

I flex my hand. It really would have felt good to hit that guy in Burger Barn. Just once.

chapter 19

communication failures of gargantuan scale

During Friday's English class, Mr. Gill drops a copy of *The Stone Angel* on each desk.

"This shouldn't be on the high school curriculum," I mumble.

Of course he hears me because English teachers have bionic ear implants, which allow them to pick up complaints about literature from two solar systems away.

"Something to say, Mr. Owens?"

"It's about an old lady." What I don't say, because for some reason I feel I should protect the other thirty students, is that the old lady dies. You'd think they could choose a more uplifting subject for the high school reading list.

"It will teach you empathy," Mr. Gill says, with a look down his nose.

The other thing I don't tell him is that my mother read this book the other year, right before I did. And when I see the cover, I picture her holding it while we sat in the waiting room of the hospital's outpatient ward. I drove her to the appointment that day, taking the afternoon off school so Dad didn't have to miss another day of work.

The way I remember it, she wasn't even reading the book. She was holding it while we waited, her fingers making nervous swirls along the cover. It would have made a good close-up shot, the smooth paper juxtaposed with the new lines on her hands.

We'd already seen her doctor. He'd told her the chemotherapy was no longer working. We could try another round, but there was only a small chance things would change.

"Is there something else we could try?" Mom asked, in a voice so professional she could have been discussing taxes with her accountant.

The doctor sighed, flipping papers as if a solution might flutter out. "We could do another drug if you want," he said. "But change is unlikely."

"If I decide against further treatment, what does that look like, exactly?" Mom asked.

This time, he at least looked her in the eye. "You'd be talking about months, not years."

Tracy was at the desk when they finally called Mom to collect her paperwork and her new appointment card. Another close-up. Hope packaged in a palm-size card.

"Tracy," Mom said, leaning across the desk a little. "If I was a relative of yours and I'd done all these treatments over the past few months . . . would you tell me to do one more round?"

I don't know if Mom knew that I'd followed her up to the desk. I don't know if she saw me, hovering by her shoulder. But Tracy saw me, and when she shook her head, she was looking at me as well as Mom.

"I can't answer that for you," she said. "Some people choose to pursue every possible treatment, and some choose to enjoy the days they have left. It's a decision you have to make for yourself, with your family."

I waited. All that afternoon, and that evening, and the next, I waited for the family discussion so I could tell her that I wanted her to do more rounds. I wanted her to do every round of chemotherapy in existence and then sign up for experimental protocols.

I wanted her to stay. I didn't want to know at what point the scales tipped, family and pain on one side, death and peace on the other. I knew that another round of chemo would mean more weeks of nausea, of lying immobile on the couch, of mouth sores and stomach cramps. But even though there was so much for her to suffer through, part of me didn't care. I wanted her to try.

"Are you with us this afternoon, Mr. Owens?" my English teacher calls.

With a start, I realize he's covered the board with notes that everyone else is copying. I pull out my notebook, but I couldn't care less about the stupid stone angel.

Mom didn't discuss her decision with her family. At least, not with me. After a week had gone by and no one had mentioned new treatments, I sat in the backyard for a long time. Just sat there on a bucked log, feeling the imprint of the wood on my ass and the prickle of the night air on my arms and waiting for the tightness in my gut to disappear. I was so mad I could have chopped that log with my bare hands, but I didn't know who to be mad at.

There were no more rounds of chemotherapy.

I spend most of lunch hour camped outside the counseling offices. Just to be clear, this is not because I need cosmic questions about life and death answered by Ms. Gladwell.

"This is a pleasant surprise. What can I do for you, Cole?"

As she breezes down the hall, Ms. Gladwell looks as fresh and carefree as a deodorant model on TV.

"I assume you're here to see me?" She smiles widely, and her eyes seem to be laughing. If it weren't so against the course of nature for a high school counselor, I would say Ms. Gladwell has developed energy. Maybe even personality.

I manage to nod.

"How is the application going?" she asks as she unlocks her office door and ushers me in. "Have you been working on your film?"

"Like a crazy person." Or like a person who might become crazy if he doesn't get into film school and is forced to live with his expanding so-called family next year. I've been filming and streaming and editing as if my life depends on it.

"Is it turning out well?" Ms. Gladwell asks.

"It's harder than I expected," I admit. People didn't say what I thought they would. I really didn't get enough useful interview material, so I've been editing with a scalpel just to extract workable lines. For the first time, I understand why Robert Flaherty fudged details in *Nanook of the North*. If people would act in normal, predictable ways, you wouldn't need poetic license. But they don't.

So far, my documentary opens with a shot of Greg speeding

down the highway outside of town. I cut to the footage of the Nester bandstand, with Hannah complaining about how hard it is to make friends in Webster. Then there's a little of Lauren's sit-in-the-ditch night and some school foyer shots. In between, with guitar instrumental in the background, there's a montage of Greg, Dallas, and Tracy looking lost, with the small town shops visible behind them. Miraculous, that part. I worked in their shots without using a scrap of what they actually said. Old Flaherty would be proud.

"Now that I've got most of the editing done, it's good," I tell Ms. Gladwell. "It has a spooky, doomed feel to it." As if we're all trapped, but not everyone realizes it. If I can swing it without seeming completely deranged, I'm going to try to end with the body of the deer. I have a few seconds of video with the deer in the foreground and the bent fender of the car barely visible in the background. . . .

"Interesting," Ms. Gladwell says, one eyebrow raised.

"I wanted to talk to you about the application. The studio needs two reference letters. My boss from my summer job will write one. Could you write the other?"

"Consider it done. No problem at all," she says.

I smile. Asking people to put your good points in writing is somewhat excruciating, and I'm relieved she said yes so easily.

"Thanks. That's great," I say.

I'm still standing there, though. The pause grows too long.

Ms. Gladwell asks, "Anything else you'd like to talk about? What's going on in your life these days?"

Briefly, I imagine telling her.

Nothing major, I'd say, except there's a stripper due to move into my house, with a baby who will be half-related to me. And my dad mentioned a few nights ago that the stripper has a small daughter as well. My life is plot twist after warped plot twist.

"Anything else?" she'd ask.

Why yes, my sort-of girlfriend has finally forced me to agree to dinner with her family. Tonight. At her mansion. Maybe we can all make small talk about my dad and the stripper.

"Nothing I really need to talk about," I tell Ms. Gladwell.

"All right. I'll get the letter done this afternoon."

A terrible thought strikes me. "Could you not sign it from the school counselor? I don't want them to think I have . . . issues."

She laughs. "I'll put it on school letterhead, and they'll assume I'm a teacher. Or I'll call myself a close personal friend." I think she actually winks at me. Winks.

"Perfect. Thank you."

Not perfect. I mean, I like Ms. Gladwell, but I absolutely

cannot have a school counselor as a close personal friend. She was joking, right? I have to get out of here before my world gets any more warped.

Deep breath. Soon, I can send off my application, then start the countdown until graduation. Sheri's baby is due in June, I've discovered. Which is ideal. I can leave town as soon as exams are over and let them have the house to themselves.

Ms. Gladwell ushers me out, leaving me in the glass fishbowl, surrounded by brochures: eating disorders, sexually transmitted diseases, homosexuality, unplanned pregnancy.

I should pick up a copy of that one for Sheri.

Just as I turn to leave, I see Lauren walking down the hallway on the other side of the glass. She's by herself, head down, shoulders slightly hunched. For the briefest moment, her elbow catches the fabric of her sweatshirt and the cotton is tugged back, stretching over her frame.

It doesn't stretch flat, like it should over someone as long and as lean as Lauren. It stretches over a bulge.

There's no mistaking it. I know Lauren's body. I mean, I *know* Lauren's body. And that swell of a belly—well, maybe that would be normal on some other girl, but not on her.

Lauren is pregnant. Like Sheri-the-stripper pregnant. Pregnant.

She looks up and catches me staring, but I don't say anything.

I can't breathe. Or move. I can only flick my eyes to her belly, then up again.

Lauren's face crumples, and she runs.

Pushing open the office door, I race after her.

"Lauren! Wait!"

She ducks into the girls' bathroom. With only a moment of hesitation, I follow.

chapter 20

pregnancy and aliens

Two girls are perfecting their mascara at the bathroom mirror.

"Cole! Get out!" they shriek in symphony. I don't look at them long enough to register who they are.

"We need a minute." There must be something urgent in my voice because they pack their makeup bags and scuttle away. This leaves me facing Lauren, who is leaning against the back wall, her arms wrapped around herself.

"Why didn't you tell me?"

She shrugs. "I tried, but you were . . . busy."

"For months? I've been busy for months?"

"You know, it's not really your problem," she says.

Not my problem. For a minute, I have this flash of hope,

like a meteor, that the baby isn't mine. I can play the role of helpful, supportive friend. But no, Lauren isn't that kind of girl. And when I look at her again, her eyes are narrowed. She's just waiting for me to ask that question.

I created a baby. I squeeze my eyes closed for a minute. The red sundress, being hungover, waking up to find Lauren's leg, naked, over mine. I remember all of that. I remember what happened in between. And it created this.

Suddenly, it's as if everything fades to black. Hannah will never speak to me again. Lauren's parents will disown her. My dad will descend into an alcoholic stupor. As for me? I may as well go home and smash my computer and my camera and shred the studio catalog. I can physically feel my chances at film school draining away.

What about Lauren? What is she expecting out of this? Out of me?

"D-do you have plans?"

I'm not supposed to say, "What are *you* planning to do?" I know that much from after-school TV specials.

She shrugs again.

"Look, I understand if you don't want me involved." Hell, at this moment I would *love* to not be involved. "But don't you think we should at least talk about this?"

Silence.

"Who else knows—besides Lex?" Obviously, Lex knows. Her behavior during the last few months finally makes sense.

Lauren stares at a bathroom stall.

"What did your parents say?" I can't believe they haven't called my dad. I would have expected Lauren's mom to be at our door with the police and/or the local exorcist the minute she found out.

Lauren keeps staring.

I'm getting a sinking feeling that all is not peachy in the state of Georgia. Assuming, metaphorically speaking, the state of Georgia is Lauren's brain and "peachy" refers to "sane."

"You haven't told your parents."

After a long pause, Lauren slowly shakes her head.

"So, who knows?"

"Lex is the only one."

Other things are now making sense. The oversize sweat-shirts. The puked pizza in Greg's car. Even the sit-in-a-ditch night, when Lauren was talking about choices and how she had choices but then she didn't have choices, and . . .

I calculate in my head. Five months, almost exactly.

"How? How have people not noticed?"

"Everyone thinks I'm depressed about the breakup. They think I'm eating too much. You should see the fridge at home— my mom's stocked it with celery sticks and low-fat yogurt."

She glances at her belly, hidden again beneath the sweat-shirt. "This . . . this would never even occur to her. She thinks I'm . . ."

"Perfect?"

Lauren pushes herself off the wall and grabs my shoulders. She stares up at me. "I need you not to tell anyone."

"Well, eventually they're going to know."

She shakes her head, a frantic look on her face. "I'm going to figure this out, Cole, but I need you not to tell."

Her eyes are not normal. She looks as if she hasn't slept in weeks. Her pupils fill up all the space between her lids. Is it possible she's pregnant *and* on drugs? Come to think of it, I'm pretty sure sitting in a ditch and smoking pot while pregnant is not doctor recommended. What the hell is she thinking?

"You can't tell," she repeats.

I nod. "Okay. I won't tell. We have to talk more, though."

She squares her shoulders and flicks her hair, then heads toward the bathroom door.

"Lauren, seriously. We have to talk."

She leaves. She's gone.

I find myself bent over, my hands on my thighs, my breath coming fast and shallow. I might vomit.

There's a yelp. A girl's voice. "What are you doing in the girls' bathroom?"

What *am* I doing in the girls' bathroom? I need help, and this is not the place to find it.

I barrel out the door and down the hall, almost smacking into Ms. Gladwell, who looks momentarily alarmed.

"Everything okay, Cole?"

I don't answer. Her brochures are not going to help me now.

Turning the corner toward the foyer, I find Lauren crying, wrapped in the arms of Hannah, of all people. I can practically hear the crash as my worlds collide. Hannah ushers Lauren toward the front doors, shooting a single "what the hell" glance at me over her shoulder as they leave. My feet stop of their own accord and my eyes scan the foyer as if searching for cover. A minute ago I was an innocent bystander. Now it seems I'm the common enemy.

I head for the side doors that lead to the parking lot. The bell is about to ring, and I find Greg exactly where I expect, leaning on his car, shoulders hunched against the cold, yammering away to Dallas.

"Long hair and a beard, like some sort of time-warped hippie," Greg's saying.

"And he just came out of your bathroom, first thing in the morning?" Dallas says.

"They pretended like he'd just stopped in for coffee. But since when does my mom have coffee guests before breakfast?"

I have no idea what they're talking about, and I don't care. I'm practically hopping from foot to foot, this secret pressing on my gut like a bladder about to burst.

"She says he makes jewelry in a studio up at the lake. An artist, apparently."

I can't wait any longer.

"Greg, can I talk to you?"

"Sure," he says.

Dallas turns to rummage in the backseat of the car, and I tilt my head toward him meaningfully. Greg shrugs.

Just as the bell rings, Dallas emerges triumphantly with a bag of chips and stuffs some in his mouth. Greg takes the bag and grabs a handful.

"Dallas, don't you have class?" I ask desperately.

"Nah," he says, licking salt off his fingers.

He's killing me. If I have to stand here for one more minute with this knowledge filling me, I'm going to pop like a human blood blister. They can feature me in a real-life ER drama.

"Greg," I say, as slowly as I can with my chest still heaving. "I have to get to class. You too, right?"

He looks at me as if I'm insane, but he hands the chips to Dallas and locks up his car. As Dallas ambles toward Canyon Street, I steer Greg around the corner of the school.

"Lauren's pregnant," I blurt. The steam from my breath hangs in the air.

"You mean Sheri's pregnant," Greg says.

"They're both pregnant!"

It's as if I'm in a 1970s film and psychedelic lines are radiating across the screen to indicate that the protagonist has lost his mind. Soon, men in white coats will rush up with gurneys and hypodermic needles.

I wish I was crazy. I wish this wasn't real.

"Lauren's pregnant. Think about it. She's been wearing extra-large T-shirts, throwing up in your car, sitting in a ditch and talking about choices. Then there's Lex's anger-management issue. How did we not see this before?"

"Dude . . . you're kinda scaring me here," Greg says.

I take a deep breath and attempt to speak at a normal speed. "Greg, you know I would believe anything you told me, right? The aliens? If you saw aliens, I would believe you."

He nods, wary.

"Lauren is pregnant." I say it slowly and deliberately. Then I lean against the cold cinder-block wall, shaking as if I just spewed my guts out.

"Pregnant," Greg repeats.

"I'm the biggest hypocrite on earth. I've been slamming

my dad for his stupidity, and here I am, the same sort of idiot. People are going to think the entire Owens family has sworn off birth control."

Lauren was careful about birth control, though. Always.

Fucking pregnant.

"We could start our own religious sect," I say. "Dad, Sheri, their baby, me, Lauren, our baby. We'll all grow dreadlocks and switch to hemp clothing."

My mind is running a million miles a minute, leaping from idea to crazy idea, trying to find somewhere safe.

"I saw a doc like that once," I tell Greg. It was called *Jonestown*. Maybe we could move our cult to Guyana and I could get a pair of mirrored sunglasses.

"Are you high?" Greg asks.

"No, I'm not high!" I'm yelling. I can't yell; I'm not supposed to be talking to anyone about this. Who knows where Lauren and Hannah went and what Lauren's telling her. They could be around the next cinder-block corner for all I know, having this same conversation.

With heroic effort, I lower my voice.

"I'm telling you, Lauren's pregnant. We slept together after we broke up. Just once. It was months ago. But she's pregnant." How many times have I repeated that phrase now? Enough to last the rest of my life, I think.

Greg's face shuts down, as if all energy has drained from him.

"I just figured it out, and she made me swear not to tell anyone," I say. "Lex is the only one who knew. The only one."

When I meet Greg's eyes, I have to take a step backward. Greg has been mad at me before. When I borrowed his remote-control car in fourth grade and lost the controller, he didn't speak to me for a week. But this look—this look is exponentially more angry.

"What?" I say. What the fuck did I do? Well, except have unprotected sex with Lauren. That was a bit of a mistake.

"THIS is what's been wrong with Lauren?" Greg is the one yelling now. "I *told* you something was wrong with her. You said it was a thyroid problem!"

"I didn't know."

"How could you not know? It's Lauren!"

This is not the reaction I was expecting. Not the reaction of a supportive friend. Greg's not on my side in this. Apparently, his crush on Lauren didn't end when she threw up in his car.

I suppose I should have anticipated this.

He pushes past me, heading back to the parking lot. A minute later, I hear the squeal of tires.

I stand there like a statue, trying to figure out what I'm supposed to do next. The final scene I'd chosen for this year— the one where I drove out of town and into the sunset—has just been cut, all the video clips deleted. But where's the alternate script?

I go back to class just for the comfort of sitting in a desk and pretending to be normal. Then my history teacher taps me on the shoulder. I look up to find the bell has rung, everyone has left, and I failed to notice.

I knock on Lauren's door after school. Her mom smiles so politely, so coldly, that you'd think I was a stranger going door-to-door for donations.

"I'm sorry, Cole. She's studying right now."

Lauren has obviously given her mother instructions. And even though she doesn't know Lauren's pregnant, her mom understands that we broke up. Not that she ever loved me in the first place.

Mrs. Michaels closes the door firmly, leaving me staring at the oak grain and the brass door knocker.

I tried catching Lauren at her locker after school. I tried calling. And now she's inside this house and I'm outside. Her poodle is barking its head off, and between the dog, her mom, and the Virgin Mary, Lauren might as well be in the witness protection program.

I drag myself back to the pickup, scuffing the thin layer of white at my feet. The snow started this afternoon, the first of the season, and I can hear kids whooping down the street, dragging sleds behind them.

I climb into the truck and slump in the seat, struggling to think logically. I've already counted the months. The time for abortion has passed—even if Lauren weren't as Catholic as the pope. So the way I see it, we have three choices. Lauren and I could get married. At one point, this would have seemed a natural choice. Now . . . well, what if I stay mad about bailing out of film school and what if Lauren's forever angry about Hannah? The whole idea seems like a sham.

Choice two: We arrange some shared system for finances. And shared system for the kid too, I suppose. It would be as if we'd gotten a divorce except without the marriage. We could still go to school, although maybe not at the same time. We could have separate careers, maybe even in separate places. This option would require both of us to act in a sane and predictable manner.

Choice three: adoption. In my mind, this is the choice that makes white lights glow and angels sing. But it's weird too. What if there's a kid out there who looks and thinks like me and he's being raised by a millionaire real estate broker and his plastic surgeon wife? Or by people who collect Star Wars figurines and name him Anakin?

My head has somehow come to rest on the steering wheel.

Anything Lauren and I choose is going to be disastrously messy. I can't see a white picket fence in sight.

Sighing, I drag myself upright and turn the ignition key. I want to go home and hibernate in the basement. Instead, I'm about to drive across town and meet Hannah's parents. I've been hoping for some sort of natural disaster—a freak avalanche blocking traffic on Canyon Street—but so far, no luck.

I saw Hannah in the hallway after school. *After* she'd seen Lauren. I tried to bail.

"I'm coming down with something," I said.

"You look fine," she said patronizingly. "I'll see you at six. We can talk after dinner—just you and me." She gave me a peck on the cheek as she breezed onward.

So now my ex-girlfriend is pregnant and not speaking to me, and my current girlfriend may or may not know that, and I'm about to meet her parents. The timing is excruciatingly bad. And the dinner itself . . . well, obviously I agreed to it in a moment of extreme emotional weakness, involving nudity on Hannah's part.

Now I'm supposed to go to her house. Her gigantic house.

It's quite possible that I've been sucked into a bleak foreign film and I can't read the subtitles. And those award-winning European movies that end up in North American theaters— they never seem to end well.

chapter 21

ditch sitting: director's cut

[Panoramic shot: *manicured hillside lawn. Camera slowly pans in on large, mansion-like house with three garages and stone urns filled with fall foliage. Pans in farther onto double oak doors at entranceway. Protagonist approaches, looking disheveled.*]

Protagonist rings bell.

DEPREZ FATHER
[*Tall, thin, graying. Wears a gray sweater vest.*]
Come in, come in. You're right on time. We like

punctuality around here. At least, I do. With two women in the family, it's generally hopeless.

[*Pair enters kitchen. Warm lighting shows rich, dark cabinets, granite countertop with fresh biscuits steaming in a basket. Matronly woman wearing apron and oven mitts turns from the stove top.*]

DEPREZ MOTHER
Cole! We've heard so much about you!

[*Mother extends oven-mitted hand, then, laughing, removes mitt. Shakes hair from her eyes. Protagonist appears shocked.*]

PROTAGONIST
We've met, actually.

MOTHER
Well, would you look at that. You're the boy who roasts his own chicken dinners. Imagine, all this time we've known each other and we didn't realize it. How did that chicken turn out, anyway?

HANNAH

[*Kissing protagonist on the cheek in greeting.*] What
are you two talking about?

MOTHER

Cole and I met in the supermarket, sweetheart.
What a coincidence! Especially since we just happen to be having roast chicken tonight. Isn't that
something? I must be psychic.

[*Protagonist looks uncomfortable. He's still smiling,
but his shoulders are hunched, and he darts glances
toward the door.*]

FATHER

Should I set the table?

MOTHER

Oh, Hannah set it hours ago. Nothing too good
for our important guest, apparently.

[*Camera pans to protagonist, who looks increasingly
panicked.*]

MOTHER

Why don't you have a seat, Cole? Pour him a
soda, would you, hon?

COLE

[*Visibly sweating.*] Thanks . . . um . . . Could I use
your bathroom?

MOTHER

Right around the corner, hon.

[*Protagonist turns and strides from the kitchen.
Camera follows him as he passes the open bathroom
door and continues to the front entrance. He leaves.
Camera flips to family members, looking stunned as
they hear the front door bang closed.*]

That's how it happened.

I went in. I freaked out. I left. I walked right out the door,
without saying good-bye to anyone and without ever talking to
Hannah.

Five minutes later, I'm sitting in the ditch down the street
from Hannah's house, hidden by the knapweed and struggling
to breathe.

Hannah's family is perfect. An hour ago, I was trying to talk to the mother of my unborn child, then I drove over here and stumbled into a Stepford family dinner.

Do people actually live like that? Did my family used to live like that?

The woman from the supermarket is Hannah's mom. The one who gave me instructions on how to roast a chicken. She's *Hannah's* mom. The lady with the breasts so big they almost touched the shopping cart handle.

Breasts. Don't think about your girlfriend's mother's breasts. There's a rule about that.

Hannah's mom's the woman with the kind eyes. I thought maybe she'd be a teacher. Or a mother of four. Actually, she *is* the mother of four. Hannah has two brothers and a sister, all in college already.

My stomach is clenched as if someone just punched me, and my ribs feel as if they're cracking. My teeth start to chatter. I realize, as I stare into the dead knapweed, the brown stalks frozen by the cold, that I've left the truck in Hannah's driveway. Which means I'm going to have to go back and get it. Which makes my stomachache worse. I can't breathe. It's possible I'm going to pass out. I put my head between my knees the way they say to do in movies and concentrate on sucking in air.

This is crazy. If I'm going to fall apart like this, I may as well go home, get drunk, and lie on the carpet with my dad. I'm sure he's collapsed there again by now.

Hannah was wearing a tight, shiny, black skirt tonight. How was I supposed to meet her dad for the first time if I kept accidentally staring at her ass? That skirt was way too tight for a family dinner. Way too tight to wear in front of a guy who just got another girl pregnant. I may never be allowed to look at Hannah's ass again. It was a bad wardrobe choice on her part. Inconsiderate.

I can hear her voice from up the road, calling my name. I sit completely still, praying she won't look for me here. It's dark now anyway. She won't be able to see outside the circle of the porch light. I can stay here all night, imagining the smells of roast chicken floating down the street, and no one will find me.

"Coooooooooole!"

When it's stretched out, my name sounds more like the fossil fuel and less like a real name. Strange I've never noticed that before.

The scene at Hannah's house replays itself in my head over and over again.

I stepped into the house. I stopped with my hand halfway extended and my mouth half open, the hearty handshake and hello I'd imagined forgotten somewhere by my tonsils. It was her. The lady from the supermarket. The one with the cooking instructions and feathered hair and huge, sagging . . .

Don't think about your girlfriend's mother's breasts.

"Well, Cole." She smiled. "I've heard lots about you and I was beginning to think I was never going to meet you. Now I see we've already met."

That's not what she said. What did she say? I can't remember her exact words, and I feel as if they might have been important.

I managed to smile and stutter and actually shake hands. Her hand—once removed from the oven mitt—was warm and dry and a little bit puffy. I looked to Hannah and back. That was her mom.

I feel as if Hannah stole her. I mean, I know that woman is not my mom. She's just someone I met in a supermarket. It doesn't matter, though. I still feel as if I had a grocery store guardian angel, a spirit guide of chicken roasting, and now Hannah's taken her away.

Hannah can keep wearing tight skirts too, and other guys—guys without babies—can enjoy the view.

The heavy feeling is back, and it's crushing. I can barely breathe with the weight of it on my ribs. I can't stand up. Just when I thought I was going to pull my life together, this baby is going to destroy everything. How can something so small do that?

Maybe I didn't have a life in the first place. Maybe in the great, cosmic blockbuster that is life on earth, I only had a walk-on part in a minor supermarket scene, and now it's been snipped from the film.

chapter 22

strategies for salvaging dignity

"Cooooooooooole!"

She's close enough to make me wince. Why doesn't she go home? At this rate, Hannah's going to call the police and issue an AMBER Alert. I can see it across the road conditions sign on the way out of town. TEEN MISSING FROM CHICKEN DINNER. On the radio, they'll add a few more details. WITNESSES DESCRIBED COLE OWENS AS POTENTIALLY UNSTABLE AFTER ATTEMPTING A FAMILY DINNER WITH A FAMILY THAT WASN'T HIS. IF YOU SEE THIS BOY, CALL THE POLICE. DO NOT APPROACH.

I don't know why I'm so freaked out. I suppose it's no big coincidence—meeting someone in a store and later finding out that you're connected. Maybe it's the idea that if I hadn't knocked

Lauren really would work things out, all on her own. And then my mom, Hannah's mom, even Hannah—they'd all be behind me. I'd never have to think about dinner, or roast chicken, or grocery stores ever again.

I have the feeling that if I examine this line of thinking, it will crack like one of these brittle knapweed stalks, but I don't care. I cling to it. I'm leaving town. No baby, or dinner, or family is going to make a difference right now. Not if it's a family who eats roast chicken together and not if it's one with a drunk dad on the living room carpet. It doesn't matter. Parenthood is a thing of the past.

"I should have raised you differently," my mom said once.

She was lying on the living room couch watching TV, wrapped in a lime-green crocheted afghan that was so ugly it was probably making her more sick just to be near it. I was sitting in Dad's recliner, balancing a plate on my lap. I'd come home from school to have lunch with her. This wasn't long before she passed away. If I'd concentrated, I probably could have seen the white lights moving in from the edges of the scene, the type of lights that movie directors use for the hereafter. As if dead people live inside clouds.

"We should have raised you Christian," she said.

I almost choked on my fried rice. We'd taken to eating

up my ex-girlfriend, Hannah's mom could have become mo
than a cameo appearance in my life. I could have created a r
for her.

In the kitchen a few minutes ago, she had lipstick on
teeth. I decide to focus on that, the hot pink smear. It makes
seem less perfect. I suppose it makes me want my mom bac
little less.

Incidentally, my mom was not round or turquoise or p
handed. She was tall—almost as tall as my dad—with ski
arms and legs, as if she were a gangly preteen who hadn't gr
into her limbs. Even her fingers were long. In soft focus,
ambient light, I can remember my dad sitting beside her o
couch, touching her fingers and saying she had piano-pl
hands. That was after she got sick. We never had a piano.

"Cole! I know you're here somewhere. Your truck's still
Stop being a lunatic."

Hannah's voice is so close I have to hold my breath.
see her through the weeds, but I can picture her standing
road with her hands on her hips, yelling into the darknes

You'd think she'd have some consideration for her
bors. They're going to run her out of town at this rate.

It'd be better if they ran me out of town instead.
willingly. I could take my almost-finished film schoo
cation. I'd rent an apartment in Vancouver. Maybe i

mostly takeout by then, Dad and I. Mom wasn't eating much anymore, although she was pretending to nibble on a spring roll just to please me.

"Christian?" I said incredulously. We'd never gone to church. Not even at Christmas and Easter like Greg's family.

"Your great-grandma and great-grandpa met in the church choir, you know."

I failed to see the relevance.

"I think it would be easier to explain things to you if we'd given you a strong faith," she said.

"Mom, I'm not a kid." Did she think we should talk about the pearly gates? Angels?

"I know. But it would be comforting. You could think of me floating around up there, wearing white."

She did. She wanted to talk about angels. As if angels could flap their wings and make us all feel better about death.

I shook my head. "I don't think that's how it works, even if you go to church."

She waved a hand in the air vaguely, brushing away the details.

Do you *believe in heaven?* That's what I wanted to ask. You'd think, after the doctors tell you there are only a few weeks left, that you would say anything and ask everything. It's not like that, though. Impending death doesn't open the Hoover Dam of communication skills. My thoughts didn't come gushing out like cold, fresh drinking water. They still stuck at the back of my throat like old sludge.

"You're not going to die." That's what I said instead. Which was stupid. We both knew she was going to die. It just seemed like the sort of thing I was supposed to say.

After a few minutes, Mom closed her eyes, worn out from the effort of our conversation. I stood up to get my bag and return to school. She called me back just as I was at the door.

"Cole. Do me a favor and clean these plates off the coffee table before you leave? If I have to stare at them all afternoon, it might kill me earlier than expected."

That time, I didn't say, "You're not going to die." But I rinsed those plates and put them in the dishwasher as if they were talismans.

It's a sad thing when you're powerless to do anything except clean the last grain of rice off a plate and wait for everything to wash into brilliant light of Hollywood's version of the afterlife.

Hannah's street has turned eerily silent. There's not even a barking dog. I can hear the faint hum of electricity in the lines overhead and the faraway drone of a truck on the highway. Slowly, I climb out of the crusty snow and brush the dirt off my ass. There are burrs on my shirt.

"Cole, are we going to talk like normal human beings?"

I freeze. "You're still here."

"Apparently."

When the hell did this girl get so tenacious? Shouldn't she have been back inside her warm and cozy dining room, tucking into a drumstick? Instead, Hannah's been patrolling the street like a stealth bot from one of Greg's video games.

"I had to . . ." There is absolutely no way to explain leaving her house. Not even to myself. "I had a stomachache."

"And you thought hiding in the bushes was the best cure for that? Didn't you hear me calling you?"

Now she's peppering me with questions like some CIA interrogator. I jam my hands in my pockets and turn toward the highway.

"You're just going to leave? My parents are totally confused."

I can't believe she expects me to stay under this sort of onslaught.

"They're going to be hurt," she says. "My mom made a roast chicken for you."

Of course she did.

I have to admit, I've been so busy wallowing in my own confused embarrassment that I haven't considered their feelings. I stop for a second, but I can't look Hannah in the eye.

"Tell her I'm sorry. Just say I had to go, okay?"

"Come back inside! Listen, I know about Lauren. I know you must be freaking out right now. Can we talk about it?"

Damn it. Why didn't Lauren tell me earlier? I've got everyone cast in the wrong roles. In my head, Lauren's the girl next door or the caring sister and Hannah's the star. Which is all wrong now. I need to recast.

"No! Okay? I can't!" I'm yelling, screaming at Hannah in the middle of the street. We may as well go and argue in the Burger Barn parking lot. It was a mistake to let Hannah into my life in the first place. I was supposed to be separating myself from Webster and now here I am, surrounded.

She's talking again, but I turn and walk away, toward the highway, my shoulders hunched in an effort to cover my ears.

I leave her sputtering. She calls after me a few more times, but she doesn't follow. I'm halfway to the highway before I realize—again—that I've left my truck in her driveway.

With every ounce of my being, I wish I could jog back to her house, meet her family, and collect my truck as if nothing crazy happened tonight. As if I didn't flip out. As if Lauren weren't pregnant. But there's a distinct lack of rewind buttons in my life right now.

I'm going to have to walk all the way to Greg's and send him to get my truck. At the moment, that's my best plan.

• • •

By Monday, Hannah and I have broken up.

There's only one small problem: She doesn't know. Friday night, I got half a dozen texts from her, with another batch in the early hours of the morning after I snuck up her driveway to collect my truck. (Greg wouldn't answer his phone, completely failing in the bail-a-brother-out department.) She e-mailed and called all weekend, then again when I didn't show up at school this morning. The girl has a serious communication dependency.

Slightly stoned from sleep deprivation and three days of dedicated TV watching, I welcome Dad home from work by heating two cans of soup and making toast. That's like a two-course dinner, which counts as fancy around here. And to celebrate the occasion, we manage to talk about nothing more stressful than the hockey scores and the weather.

When we're finished, Dad retreats to the living room. The phone rings.

"Don't answer it!" I yell. He was out for most of the weekend. He hasn't heard about my new phone policy yet. (#1. Don't answer it.)

Dad doesn't ask questions.

By the time the dishes are done, the phone has rung three or four more times and I have steadfastly ignored it. I set about rinsing and recycling Dad's collection of beer bottles. There are seventy-three.

Afterward, I lean on the door frame and watch as his snores literally shake the recliner.

There are six more beers in the fridge.

I consider pouring them down the drain while he's passed out. Then I have a better idea. I retrieve my backpack from downstairs and load them all inside.

They clink against my back as I stride down the hill toward Greg's house. I've gone about three steps when Hannah's Saturn idles up beside me and she rolls down the window. Damn. The girl must have been on surveillance duty. There should be stalking laws against that sort of thing.

"Hey, handsome," she says, her breath steaming into the cold air. "Thought you might want a ride." Her eyes are red, a contradiction to her wavering smile. Even with puffy skin, though, she's gorgeous.

A ride is the last thing I want. In fact, if the route to Greg's house was lined with hot coals and I was barefoot, I would still rather walk. I can't get into a car with a gorgeous girl who is not the mother of my future child.

"I need the exercise," I say.

The smile disappears. "Look, Cole. You don't have to talk to me after today if you don't want to. But you owe me this. Get in the damned car."

This is not the voice of Home Base Hannah.

I climb in the car.

"Do you have any idea how hard this is for me?" she asks.

I'm not exactly having the time of my life either.

"I wasn't born here like the rest of you. I know that you and Lauren have a lot to work out right now, but I don't have a thousand friends to turn to once you dump me."

The word "dump" is a little harsh.

"It's not like I planned this," I snap.

"You and I are so good together. It's just not fair." Blinking fast, holding her lips tight, Hannah is trying not to cry. I appreciate the effort. There's nothing worse than being trapped in a moving car with a crying girl.

"This town sucks," she says.

"Agreed."

Then Hannah's breath catches. When a tiny hiccup of a sob escapes, I feel something crumble in my chest. Life has seriously screwed with me this week, and I'm taking it out on her. "I'm sorry," I tell her. "I really, really am. But there's stuff I have to figure out."

"You don't have to do it by yourself."

I sigh. It's not that help wouldn't be nice. But I'm at the bottom of a ditch here. The stinking, slimy, toxic-waste-coated bottom of a ditch. I'm so far in that I can't see the tops of the banks anymore. It doesn't feel fair to pull someone down here with me.

She puts a hand on my leg. "I could help you. We could figure it out together."

As romantic as that prospect sounds, it's not going to work. She knows it too. I can see it in her face.

"Can you just drop me off?" I ask.

Hannah snatches her hand back. She wraps her fingers around the steering wheel, and I watch as her knuckles turn white.

"So that's it," she says.

"Sorry."

I really am, not that Hannah believes me. I'm sorry for hurting her, sorry for running out on her parents. Most of all, I'm sorry for my damned self right now.

She leaves me on the side of the road by the hospital, close to Greg's house.

"Check yourself into the psych ward while you're here," she shouts out the window before pulling away with all the power her Saturn can muster.

For a few minutes, I stand on the corner letting the wind cool my head and waiting for the tight feeling in my throat to pass. Across the street from the hospital, there's an old Lutheran church with a looming brown cross in front and one of those marquees that declare the scripture for the next week's service.

I AM WITH YOU ALWAYS, it says, EVEN UNTO THE END OF THE WORLD.

"That's half the problem!" I yell. I should go over there and kick that sign. Do churches put them up specifically to torment people? "Why can't everyone leave me alone?"

Now I'm yelling at a sign while standing by myself in the dark.

To make things worse, when I finish yelling, I discover that I'm not actually alone. Tracy is having a smoke outside the door to the emergency room.

She waves me over, and since my better judgment has already deserted me, I join her, motioning for a drag of her cigarette. As I cough, she examines me with a pursed lip. A pierced, pursed lip. Seeing a thick silver stud on the lip of a forty-year-old Webster nurse is like seeing a UFO.

"You wanna talk about it?" she says.

Yeesh. Is there some sort of estrogen-based conspiracy around here? No, I don't want to talk about it! And if I did, she probably *would* check me into the psych ward.

I bet they have good drugs in the psych ward. It's tempting, but not quite as tempting as my next idea.

"Maybe later," I tell Tracy, passing back her smoke. "I gotta go."

I turn toward town and text Greg as I walk. I still have the beer. He can pick me up.

chapter 23

the binge

Greg is pissed. Somewhere between fleeing Hannah's house, amputating my girlfriend from my life, and acting like a lunatic in front of the church, I forgot about the part where I impregnated Greg's future wife. He, apparently, has not forgotten.

"C'mon, bud." Since he refused to answer the phone or the door (a trend among my friends these days), I've taken to standing outside his bedroom window and yelling. "I know you're in there. I saw you close the curtains."

No response.

"Can we talk about this? Over a drink? Or two?"

I'm having déjà vu. Only a few months ago, I knocked on

Greg's window to tell him that Lauren and I had broken up. He was more helpful then.

"I didn't do any of this on purpose. I could really use some help figuring it out. . . ."

The curtains whip back and I jump. With a creak, the window slides open and Greg sticks out his head.

"You want us to figure out something? What kind of something?"

"I don't know. Do we have to talk about it here?"

He tilts his head, considering. "Yes."

"What do *you* think I should do? Ask her to marry me? Get a job in Vancouver and mail child-support checks? I don't know, man. This doesn't even seem real yet, and I can't get past the prison guard to talk to Lauren."

"You haven't talked to her?" He makes it sound like a felony.

"Not since she told me."

"Nice. Why don't you start with that, Cole? It's good to have goals."

He slams the window shut.

"She won't let me in!"

Inside the house, music starts to blare. The panes vibrate.

I swear, these people are trying to drive me insane. They're like octopuses when I want to get rid of them. Octopi? Creatures with big frickin' tentacles that won't let go. And now, when I could actually use some help, they disappear into the dark depths of their own worlds. Bottom-feeders, all of them.

Unwilling to go home, I head down the hill toward 7-Eleven. That's where I find Dallas.

He slaps me on the back as if I'm the prodigal friend. "How's it going? Where's the rest of the gang?" For some reason, his accent makes me feel better. I can't talk to Dallas without expecting cowboys to ride by and oil rigs to gush in the background.

"Hannah and I broke up. And Greg's sulking in his bedroom like a chick."

Dallas doesn't ask more questions, which I appreciate.

"Y'all got time for a drink?"

He doesn't ask questions *and* he wants to have a beer with me on a Monday night. "Dallas," I say, returning his shoulder slug, "it's possible you're my soul mate. I have half a dozen beers in my pack."

The drinks slide down surprisingly quickly in the alley behind the store. When they're gone, we go in search of a new supply.

An evening in the Prospector bar is risky because even if the bartender isn't some guy who graduated two years ago and knows

I'm still not of age, there are always a dozen customers who can identify me.

Tonight, I really don't care.

"We're grown men," I tell Dallas as we push open the heavy double doors.

"Captains of our own ships," he agrees.

Fortunately, there's a middle-aged woman tending bar. She has long, red hair pulled into a thick braid and looks like a Wild West pioneer. No matter. She doesn't know us, and she doesn't blink when we order two beers. Then two shots of tequila. Then two more beers. When Dallas slaps down a twenty to pay for the next round, she only raises her eyebrows in a way that suggests she'll be laughing later, when we're puking our guts out.

"She underestimates us," I tell Dallas.

"Because we're men of purpose," he says.

"Men of independent means."

"Makers of our own destinies!" he says grandly, spilling some of his beer as he hoists it.

That's when Dad sits down beside us.

We freeze. Usually you can predict what a parent is going to do in a certain situation. If Greg's mom had just spotted us, for example, we would be marching home to the beat of a lecture on the mind-bending effects of alcohol and the cancerous toxins released in our bloodstreams.

With Dallas's dad, there would have been a slow wink, a head tilt toward the door, and a deep, "Git your asses on outta here."

My dad? I have no idea what he's going to say. And I don't think he knows either. For what seems like a long time, the three of us sit silently staring at one another. Finally, he takes a deep breath and blows it between pursed lips. Then he raises a hand to the bartender and holds up three fingers.

"Guess you're gonna grow up sometime, eh, boys?" he says.

When the beer arrives, we clink the tops of the bottles like we're old buddies and slurp in unison.

Since we arrived, the bar has filled with a strange, Monday night mix of after-shift loggers and committed drinkers. Despite the new beer, I'm uncomfortable.

I find myself wishing Dad had kicked us out.

Dallas, a grin on his face the size of the Rio Grande, has crossed the room to play pool with a group of loggers. The way he's lipping them off, he's going to get thrown out on his ass soon.

I stay on my stool, struggling to think clearly. After repeated attempts to focus, I hit on the problem. I would like to be the type of guy who handles things better than this and without the help of alcohol. Didn't I recently tell my dad that things had to change? My negotiating power is draining like a spilled beer. Sheri's pregnant. Lauren's pregnant. Drinking with Dad, it's like I've signed on to the "if you can't beat 'em, join 'em" team. And

"See? First my head moves. Then, a while later, my eyesh see you." I hear the slur, and I'm about to repeat myself—to ensure I'm making this completely clear—when I'm distracted by Ms. Gladwell's friend. It's Tracy. Tracy's holding hands with Ms. Gladwell.

If seeing a goth nurse in Webster is like seeing a UFO, this is like seeing a UFO actually abduct someone.

"Hey! You two are leshbians," I tell them. "That's cool."

I don't want them to be uncomfortable.

I point a finger toward Ms. Gladwell. "This explains a lot. You've kinda changed."

They're both looking at me with the same bemused expression that Tracy wore outside the hospital a couple hours ago.

"I mean that in a good way," I clarify. I'm finding it difficult to look at them out of both eyes at once. My right eye is spontaneously closing.

I experiment. "Camera one. Camera two."

"Cole, how 'bout we take you home?" Tracy says. "My truck's just down the block."

"Nah, I'll walk," I tell her. "Last time I got in the car with a woman, it washn't good. Not good at all."

"We could call your dad to come get you," Ms. Gladwell suggests.

"He's inside," I say.

in a few hours, we'll both stagger up to the house, where we'll lean against the wall and scrape our keys against the door frame searching for the lock.

There's something not right about that.

I stand abruptly, which sends the bar spinning around me. "Be right back," I mumble, heading in the general direction of the bathroom. Halfway there, I'm distracted by a blast of cold air from the front door. It's like a slap in the face, in a good way.

I don't realize how noisy the bar was until I emerge. Out here, it's perfectly silent and still. The cloudless sky is spread with stars. It's cold for November—deep-winter cold—but I linger, unwilling to go back inside and talk to my dad. As long as I hover here or lean against the frigid brick wall, I'm in limbo, absolved from all decision making.

The crunch of footsteps on snow echoes through the empty street. I hear women's voices, punctuated by a peal of laughter.

When I turn my head, there's a three-second delay in my vision. There must be a traffic jam inside my brain between the optical nerves and whatever lobe is responsible for interpreting vision.

"Cole?" Ms. Gladwell spots me against the bricks. She's holding hands with a woman. I'm pretty sure I'm not imagining things.

"Watch," I tell her. Then I turn my head toward her friend

Their eyebrows go up in unison.

"What if I get him?" Tracy says. "Then you can both head home together?"

"I don't think that's a good idea."

A sand truck approaches from the far end of the street, its yellow lights swirling. The way those lights reflect on the snow . . . hypnotizing. I should work that into a science doc somehow.

"You should really go home," Tracy says.

"Yeah, all right, but I'll get my dad. If you go in there, you might get beat up. It's that whole UFO thing, you know?"

She looks baffled. I'm about to explain, but Ms. Gladwell takes my shoulders and points me toward the stairs.

"You go and get him," she says. "We'll wait."

chapter 24

scenes of gratuitous violence

I swing open the wooden door and immediately duck a punch. And when I stop to congratulate myself on showing such high-level agility in my inebriated state, I get elbowed in the eyeball. Pain radiates through my skull. Immediately, my fists are swinging. With one eye open and the other watering like a garden sprinkler, it takes a few tries before I connect. There's a satisfying crunch and a yell. I can hear my own breath as I suck air between my teeth. Adrenaline races through me and even though I know someone else just punched my cheekbone, I barely feel it. I swing again and again.

"I've called the police!" The bartender is screaming to be heard above the ruckus.

For a brief moment, Dallas's face appears. He grins at me with blood in his teeth, and then we're both back in the fray. It's spectacular, really. Everything in rough cut. I jab right and duck a swing, elbow left for room, let another punch fly. There's something hugely gratifying about this. Each connected throw sends triumph through me. It's so much better than getting blindsided in the girls' bathroom by your pregnant ex-girlfriend. I think of the recent fights that I *could* have had . . . that terrible dad at Burger Barn, for example. Why didn't I go for it?

Then I get hammered in the gut. The breath whooshes from me and I fold in half. A kick to the ribs flattens me further.

I hear the bartender shouting again, but from my current doubled-over position, I can't see her through the jumble of legs and arms. The way I picture it, she's standing on the bar with a double-barreled shotgun, her feet firmly planted and her braid slung over one shoulder. It's possible I've staggered my way into a western movie.

As a siren wails outside, I watch Dallas's boots move closer to me. He's still kicking and swinging.

Suddenly, there's a shatter of glass, a shower of shards around me, and a stream of swearing above my head.

Managing to suck in some oxygen, I push my way upright.

Dallas is holding his wrist, and blood is squirting—literally squirting—from between his fingers. The swearing's coming partly from him and partly from the loggers, who've all stepped back in unison. A bar fight turned square dance.

I scan the crowd for my dad, but I can't spot him.

The door swings open. I expect the cops, but it's Ms. Gladwell. She grabs my arm and hauls me outside.

"But Dallas—" I protest. "There's crazy blood. . . ."

"Tracy," she calls over her shoulder. "They've got room for your skills in there."

Tracy's already stepping around us, shoving her way inside.

The cop is only a moment behind. He stops to shoot a questioning look at Ms. Gladwell. One that asks, "What am I about to find?"

"I think it's mostly over," she tells him. I wait for him to question me next, maybe ask for my ID. He doesn't even glance in my direction. I guess an underage drunk is not at the top of his list at the moment.

"Okay, now we're taking you home, Cole," Ms. Gladwell says after the cop's gone inside.

"My dad. And Dallas . . . ," I protest.

Another siren pierces the night, and an ambulance barrels down the street. Looks like Dallas will be getting a ride too.

"Tracy'll take care of Dallas. I'll check on him after I drop you off. Unless you want that cop to throw you in the drunk tank for the night with the rest of the guys in there?"

Is there really a drunk tank? Either way, it gets my feet moving.

I make it all the way home without puking in Tracy's truck, which I consider a major accomplishment.

"Thanks," I tell Ms. Gladwell as she pulls up in front of the house. Then, just as I'm about to slide out the door, "I know Tracy from the hoshpital." I hear myself slur again, and I concentrate hard to make the rest of the thought come out clearly. "From when my mom was sick."

"I know." She nods.

I put one hand on her shoulder and look her in the eye, as if I'm the local relationship guru. "She's a good one. I'm happy for you."

Once she's gone, I spend quite a long time facedown on my mattress, with one hand gripping the headboard to make the room stop spinning. What seems like hours later, Dad sits on the side of my bed. It's such an unusual occurrence, I manage to lift an eyelid.

"You're not in the drunk tank," I say.

"The drunk tank. Is there really such a thing?"

"I've wondered that myself."

"I stayed out of the way," he says. "Was worried about you, though. I couldn't find you."

Looking at the world out of one eye is discombobulating.

I let my lid drop closed and tighten my grip on the headboard.

"You shouldn't have been in the Prospector tonight," Dad says.

In a stating-the-obvious contest, that one would win first prize. I grunt in agreement.

After a long break, during which I hear myself snore once or twice, Dad says, "I guess I shouldn't have been there either."

Interesting, that. Does he mean that he should have taken me home? Or that he shouldn't have been in the bar on a Monday night?

I'm still considering the question when I pass out.

Hopefully, I don't miss any more of Dad's deep thoughts.

The blast of alarm clock music and the sunlight slicing between the curtains feel like Guantanamo Bay interrogation techniques. I curl into a fetal position and shield my head. Under direct torture, I might admit that four beers, a couple shots of tequila, and a few more beers are well past my drinking tolerance. Someone may or may not have tossed his cookies outside the back door early this morning, having gotten confused about the direction of his own bathroom.

That may or may not have been me.

What was I thinking?

When I turn my head, my vision still follows on a three-second delay. If you factor in the horrendous music blaring from my alarm, I could be inside a film shot in freeze frames.

Snap. Guy sprawled in bed. *Snap.* Guy pushing himself upright on side of bed. *Snap.* Guy making desperate grab for desk-side garbage can. *Snap.* Guy heaving.

Maybe I am in Guantanamo. Maybe they're trying to break me with strobe lights.

My eyes focus on the red digits of the clock.

If I'm not in prison, I have exactly twelve minutes to get to school.

I could stay in bed. I waste one minute considering that option. Positive side: I'd be in bed. Negative sides: Ms. Gladwell might call the house—exactly the sort of thing a teacher would do to make you die of embarrassment; if Dad's still home, I'll have to talk to him; I would be acknowledging to myself that I'm the kind of guy who gets wasted at the bar on a Monday night.

I might make it on time if I leave immediately. I will likely be late if I change my clothes and brush my teeth.

I decide it's worth the risk. Brushing my teeth at this moment is basically an antiterrorism measure.

I manage to dress myself and spend an extra few minutes admiring my shiner in the mirror. It's mostly black, with a tint of purple. If I had six-pack abs and a few tattoos, I'd look like the latest mixed-martial-arts champion.

"Champion" is possibly not the best word to describe me right now.

I make it all the way to school, check in with the secretary, and start down the hallway. Then I have to make an abrupt turn into the waiting area of the counseling office to dry heave in a garbage can.

When I finish, Ms. Gladwell is standing behind me, leaning on the door frame. To my satisfaction, she looks a little rough herself.

"Cole, what are you doing here? Go home."

"I think . . ." The end of the sentence escapes me. If she's not going to call and check up on me, then what the heck *am* I doing here? Dad's probably already at work. And what difference does one Tuesday of school make?

"Is Dallas okay?"

"Tracy said they stitched him up. He'll be fine."

I nod, which almost makes me heave again. "I guess I'll go home."

I don't, though. Since I'm already awake and at least somewhat ambulatory, I drag my butt up the hill to the hospital. I don't even have to ask for directions to Dallas's room—I find him sitting on a bench outside the ER, fingers tucked into his armpits for warmth and head tilted back against the wall. If I look as if I've been through Guantanamo and Ms. Gladwell looks as if she's had a one-night stand, Dallas looks approximately a billion times worse. His hair is standing entirely on end. One cheek is swollen, he has a black eye, and his arm's in a hospital-issue, puke green sling.

"I hear they sewed you up," I say.

"Thirty-seven stitches. I just got discharged."

"Shouldn't you go home to bed?"

"And waste these good drugs?" he asks, hauling his head upright and grinning. "I saw a pink elephant dancing in midair this morning, dude. Seriously."

"Nice." It sounds like an improvement on my morning.

"Hey, where'd you go last night, Cole? You left me at the hospital with some vampire nurse."

"She's all right. Her name's Tracy."

"Yeah, but where were you? You were my wingman, and then you disappeared like a rattlesnake in a thunderstorm."

"Do rattlesnakes disappear in thunderstorms?"

Dallas glares at me.

"Sorry, man."

"You don't go to the bar and then scoot your ass out when the fight starts."

"Are you seeing this eye? I was there!"

"Well, all I'm sayin' is you shoulda been there afterward."

"All right, I should have gone to the hospital. But Ms. Gladwell dragged me home."

"What the hell was Ms. Gladwell doing in the bar?"

"She wasn't . . . I don't know. Anyway, sorry."

He's probably right—I should have followed him to the hospital. I'm just not sure I can take responsibility for any more people in this town. If my life were a screenplay, every role would be filled and casting irrevocably closed.

"Well, I'll tell y'all one good thing," Dallas says.

"What?"

"I got an idea."

This should be interesting.

"All those white sheets draped everywhere got me thinking. Toga party. Ten days from now, last Saturday of the month. What do you say?"

"I think you're the only guy I know who ends up in a hospital and spends his time planning a toga party."

Dallas looks smug.

Eventually, I ask how he's getting home. "I can go get the truck," I offer.

He shakes his head. "My dad's inside doing paperwork. He's not too happy at the moment."

This seems like my exit cue. After promising to work on a

toga, I stagger off in the direction of home, using my remaining mental abilities to keep my feet moving. If I had more brain-power left over, I might think about the words that keep rattling around my head. "You don't go to the bar and then scoot your ass out when the fight starts," Dallas said. There's something to that.

If I weren't so hung over, I could figure it out.

chapter 25

downhill on a downhill slope

I'm sweating inside my ski jacket, feeling mildly carsick and mindlessly etching the word "condoms" into the back of the leather bus seat. School buses haven't changed since my fourth-grade field trip to Fort Trapp, where we ate lard sandwiches and panned for gold. The air still smells like a mix of gas and disinfected puke.

We're on our way to Whitedome, in Logan. I agreed to this ski trip a month ago because Greg was in charge of organizing it for the French teacher (which explains his A in French last term). Back then, Greg was actually speaking to me. Now he's enthroned at the back of the bus and surrounded by girls, and the trip doesn't sound so appealing. Especially as Lex is sitting right behind me and giving me the evil eye through the seat. Or so I imagine.

Still, the fact that she's back there, without Lauren for once, gives me an idea. When the bus is sufficiently chaotic, I turn and poke my head around.

"Where's Lauren today?" I ask her.

"She's not up to skiing right now," Lex says pointedly.

"But what's she doing?"

"Hannah's taking her shopping." The way she says it makes me think she's not entirely pleased. Which might work to my benefit.

"Lex, you know Lauren better than anyone. Do you think she and I could have a conversation through you?"

"What are you, six?" she snaps. Her seatmate giggles.

"She won't talk to me. If I stop her in the hall, she stands like a zombie until I go away."

"Then learn to read body language," Lex says. "She doesn't want to see you."

I ignore that. "Her mom screens her phone calls. I've left her notes, and she hasn't replied."

"Not my problem."

"Lex, it's my problem. I'm asking for your help."

She examines her fingernails for a few moments before looking at me. "I'll think about it," she says finally. "Don't get your hopes up."

I slide back down in my seat, and something in my chest loosens, just a notch. Lex might actually help me, which would be progress. Serious progress. On a scale of one to ten, my urge to throw myself off the bus has dropped to a 9.5.

A month ago, I could have comforted myself thinking that skiing could be a useful career skill. If my films were shown at the Sundance Film Festival, for example, I could be one of those directors in a faux-fur-lined jacket and dark sunglasses, waving to the paparazzi between screenings and ski runs.

That's how I first heard about *Uganda Rising* and Alison Lawton—because I was reading about past winners at Sundance. The film is all about a part of Uganda where kids got stolen from their families and turned into child soldiers for the rebel army.

The movie made Lauren nauseous. I remember exactly what she said:

"They're in Africa!"

"And?"

"I can't fix Africa. I can't fix it. I can't do anything at all about it, and now I'm going to feel sick all day thinking about those children. What good does that do?" She was blinking fast.

She had a point. But when I suggested that we go to Uganda and make follow-up documentaries to raise awareness or funding, Lauren thought the idea was ridiculous. And that, apparently, made me angry enough to break up with her.

Indirectly, Alison Lawton is responsible for the demise of my relationship with Lauren, our post-relationship one-night stand, and my current predicament. I wonder if she feels bad about that?

With a belch of exhaust, the bus finally rounds the last bend to the summit of the Logan-Webster, highest year-round highway in the world. There's a frozen lake to our right and avalanche-control stations down the slope to the left. Straight ahead, this road leads all the way to Vancouver.

Probably, I should hijack the bus, kick everyone off, and just keep driving.

This thought grows more appealing as behind me, Lex and her friend start giggling, something about sausage wieners.

I huddle in my seat and close my eyes. It's unfortunate that humans have eyelids but no earlids. If early man had ever had to sit in front of Lex on a school bus, he would have evolved earlids.

My mind wanders. I ate wieners for dinner last night. Wieners and boxed mac and cheese, in silence, with my dad. Since the bar fight, we've been tiptoeing around each other, talking only about the blandest of subjects: food choices, the location of the truck keys, whether a brown shirt goes with gray pants. (We didn't reach a conclusion on that last one.) As far as I can tell, Dad hasn't been back to the bar. He's been spending his evenings alternately watching the History Channel and Clint Eastwood movies. Sober.

It's kind of scary, actually.

With a grinding of brakes, the bus arrives in the Whitedome parking lot. We stumble down the steps in our ski pants and jackets, like a string of multicolored marshmallows. The air is cold enough to sear my lungs.

Near the rental hut, I stop and make a show of adjusting the Velcro on my cuffs. Really, I'm waiting for Greg. I find it hard to believe—no matter what else is throwing the universe out of whack—that we're not going to ski together.

He almost walks past me, chatting away to some girl in a hot pink ski suit. Then he stops and sends her ahead.

"Tons of powder," he says.

"Tons."

"They're setting records for the snowpack already."

"I heard that too."

I scuff a boot against the icy trail of footprints. Part of me wants to apologize for screwing things up, but I haven't actually fixed anything with Lauren since the last time I said I was sorry. It feels wrong to apologize again before sorting things out.

Greg opens his mouth to say something. Then someone calls to him from the other side of the hut. There's a whole group there, beckoning.

"I'm sorta surprised you're here," Greg says. He's already turning toward the others.

"I thought we'd . . ." But what am I going to say? *I thought you'd hang out with me instead of those other people?* That sounds lame. Besides, if I weren't me, I wouldn't want to hang out with me either.

"I guess I'll see you up there," I say.

Greg raises his hand in acknowledgment as he crunches his way across the snow.

I join the lineup at the rental shop and pretend to be interested in conversation with a bunch of guys from the junior volleyball team. By the time we're matched with skis and sent out into the snow, I've expended my entire stock of small talk and socialization tactics.

"You coming, Cole?" one of them calls as they head to the chairlift.

"I have to adjust a binding. Go ahead, I'll catch up."

I wait until the entire group has gone up the lift. Then, when it's all strangers, I fall into line. I get on the chair with an older man, and we ride silently to the summit.

Once there, even the strangers swooping back and forth across the slope seem like too much company. I follow the tree line until I find a single set of ski tracks through the trees. Plowing into the powder, I focus on twisting between evergreens.

Knees bent, arcing back and forth around mounds of snow and sweeping boughs. Other than the soft swish of my skis, it's blissfully quiet. Peaceful. Blank. Back and forth, back and forth, I pick up speed and twist faster and . . .

The problem with blindly following someone else's tracks is that someone else may be a better skier. Without warning, the twin lines disappear over a precipice. They swoosh right on through the snow and out into nothingness. For a split second, I consider going over. I can see it, Warren Miller sports-action style: my body flying through the air, skis perfectly parallel, poles steady, tips up in preparation for landing. It'll be shot from multiple angles: a helmet cam, a stationary cam behind me, and an aerial shot from the helicopter. . . .

Fuck.

I don't ski *that* well.

At the last possible moment, I throw my weight to the side, one ski lifting off the snow and the other carving a deep rut in the ice at the edge of the drop. I get a glimpse of sky and snow below, and then I'm careering uncontrollably sideways toward the evergreens along the edge and . . .

Falling.

Not into complete nothingness. One ski flips off and another twists down—with me attached—to stick like a toothpick into the snow. The back of my head smacks hard against a patch of ice.

The world is suddenly, eerily silent.

When I look around, I'm under one of the evergreens, in a well where the bushy green boughs have prevented the snow from falling. The hole is about twice as wide as my body and deeper than my height. Even with one ski stuck straight down below me, the lip of the snow is still above my head. My elbows and knees are wedged into the sides, holding me upright. Basically, I'm stuck in a vertical cave of ice.

Some help would be good right about now.

If this were a film, the edges could bleed to white and my mom's ghost would appear, pushing aside some branches and perching on the lip of my icy well, swinging her snowsuit-clad legs.

I blink. A film version of my mom is not going to get me out of here. I must have really whacked my head. Scrabbling my hands higher, searching for a way to pull myself out, I cause another mini-avalanche of snow. Cold trickles down the back of my neck.

"Looks like you're stuck," my film mom would say.

"Just resting."

"This is exactly why they don't recommend skiing by yourself," she'd continue, still swinging her feet. Music would swell in the background because this would be an epiphany of sorts. A teaching moment in the world of Disney family flicks.

A sprinkle of ice chips falls on my face, an effect I consider shockingly realistic. I guess even melodramas are coming in 4-D these days.

"If you ask me—" she'd say.

"Which I didn't. Because you're sort of . . . dead."

"Completely a figment of your imagination," she'd agree.

I reach to finger the bump on the back of my head. It hurts like hell. "Unless I'm dead too."

"I always pictured the afterlife to be less icy," she'd say.

She would know, I suppose.

"Shouldn't your friends be here? Don't you watch out for each other?"

Ignoring those questions, I swing one leg to the side, trying to snap off my ski. It works, eventually. Once my boot is free, I start searching for a toehold.

My head pounds. Every few minutes, I have to stop and rest it against the ice. I almost wish my dead mother really were here because then the film could cut to when I woke up in bed, knowing the fall was all a bad dream.

Another toehold attempt. Another rest.

A word of encouragement would be good right now. A supportive smile. There was always something inexplicably comforting about my mom's presence. She's sort of reassuring even when she's an advice-spouting illusion.

"I miss you," I say out loud.

There you go: One crack on the head and I'm talking to dead people.

If I want to get out of this hole, I'm going to have to climb. I jab my foot backward and finally, I manage to chip a hold in the ice. Balancing on that heel, I haul upward and swing an arm over the lip of the tree well. Then I stop to pant.

"Totally going to be okay here," I say to my mom. "No need for you anymore. We can go right to the cut scene."

"I could leave, son, but it looks as if you could use a little help."

Interesting. That's not my mother's voice. It's an older man's. And he's wearing a bright red jacket and staring down at me. Ski patrol. He probably thinks I'm a lunatic. There's a younger guy behind him, also staring.

"I'm fine," I mutter. "I was just about to climb out."

As the young one pulls out a radio, I take a furtive look around. She's not there, of course. And even though I know she was never there, her absence leaves me a little hollow inside.

I try to tug myself farther onto the snow, but my foot slips. Only the old guy's hand, now clamped around my shoulder, keeps me from falling back into the hole.

"Thanks," I mumble. "I would have gotten out, probably. I was just sort of missing my mom."

What the . . . ? Why am I talking about her with strangers? I must seriously have a brain injury.

"We'll give her a call, soon as we get you down the mountain," he says.

"Good luck with that," I tell him.

The ski patrol team straps me onto a stretcher for the ride down. I gaze skyward as branches and chairlift cables whip by me. By the time we finally slide to a stop, I think my eyelids have frozen open.

"Let's get you inside," the older one says.

From my upside-down position, I see the Swiss-Alps-style gingerbread of the hut, then the wood-paneled ceiling.

"Got yourself into a bit of a mess there," says the young guy. He seems to be one of those people with a talent for stating the obvious. "Ah, well. Happens to most of us at some time or another."

"That's what we're here for," says the older one.

Then, while one of them takes my blood pressure and the other radios to find the adult responsible for me, I realize something: We all *do* get ourselves into messes. A lot of messes.

I blink on command and obediently follow a penlight with my eyes. The whole time, I'm cataloging people who have messed up. There's Lauren, obviously. Trying to seem in control when, really, she's never been more confused. And Hannah, with her oh-so-casual act when she desperately wants to fit in. There are more. Lex. Greg's mom. Greg's dad.

My dad.

Maybe he fell in a metaphorical tree well when Mom died and he's still trying to pull himself out. I assumed he had some sort of master plan, even if it was to become a committed drunk. But no, he's been flailing around like the rest of us, searching for footholds.

"I think you're all right," the younger ski patrol guy says. "Probably a mild concussion. You might feel some dizziness in the next few days, and you'll definitely have a headache. Check in with your doctor when you get home."

Lauren. Hannah. Greg. My dad. A concussion is the least of my problems.

"Buddy," I tell him, "I have a lot of headaches. What's one more?"

chapter 26

experimental treatments for post-traumatic stress syndrome

It turns out that being rescued by ski patrol does not actually cause you to die of embarrassment. Which is unfortunate because in a choice between death and that bus ride home, during which half the bus (girls) gushed over me and the other half (guys) mercilessly mocked me, I would have chosen death. Hands down.

I am so relieved to get home. So relieved, I can't even describe the level of relief that I feel. I want to dump my ski stuff, crawl into bed, and stay there until January.

"I'm here," I yell in the direction of the living room. "I'm going to bed."

"Don't go yet; we haven't said hello!"

Seriously? I would pay a million dollars just to go to bed without anyone talking to me, and I have to hear *that* particular voice in my house?

Well, it could be worse. I could still be chatting with my dead mother.

Or maybe that would be better.

"Cole!" Sheri smothers me in a hug that squishes her breasts against my ribs in a highly uncomfortable way. She reeks of gardenias and she's wearing a black dress that's splattered with massive red flowers that look like vaginas.

I should have known she was here. I should have smelled her as soon as I walked in the door.

"I have a headache. I have to go to bed." It's worth a try.

"A headache! I'll make you some tea. First, we have something to tell you. Come. Come!"

I have no choice. She drags me by the arm as if I'm a stuffed bear she won at the fair. The vagina fair. I really can't look at her dress.

My dad—my big, square-shouldered, lumberyard dad—is sitting at the kitchen table with shimmering stickers all over his cheeks. He appears to be doing crafts with a small, pigtailed child.

Maybe I should have asked the ski patrol guys for some meds.

"Cole! We've been waiting for you," Dad says. "This is Brittany Anne."

The little girl looks up at me and smiles, pigtails swinging and glitter dotting her nose. She's a miniature version of Sheri, except less smelly and with better fashion sense.

"Hey," I manage.

"Want to make a paper snowman?" she asks. "We have glitter."

I sit down at the table, partly because it's hard to say no to a small child with glitter, but mainly because if I don't sit down, I'm going to keel over. After a minute, once Brittany Anne has equipped me with my own construction paper and a supply of white glue, I look up to see both Dad and Sheri beaming at me.

"What?" I say.

"Brittany Anne is Sheri's daughter," Dad says.

"I figured that."

"She's five. She usually lives in the Okanagan."

"My sister helps me out there," Sheri explains.

"We think she's going to like it here, though." Dad has stood up and moves to put an arm around Sheri's waist.

"Cole . . ."

I'm frozen with the green glitter jar in one hand and the glue bottle in the other. If I had been thinking, I should have been sniffing it to handle this conversation.

"You have glitter on your forehead." Sheri giggles.

"Cole, Sheri's quit her job. She's going to look for something involving less . . . travel. I've asked Sheri to marry me."

"That rhymes," Brittany Anne says.

"And to move in here," Dad continues.

"Get it? Sheri and marry?" Brittany Anne says.

I am trying to breathe. Really, I'm trying.

This is a complete betrayal of my mother. Dad mourned for slightly over a year before proposing to a pregnant exotic dancer with a preexisting child, and now both stripper and child are going to move into my mother's house.

"You look kinda sick," Brittany Anne tells me.

At that moment, the phone rings. Sheri grabs it as if she already lives here. "Owens residence," she coos.

"Oh, my." Her voice drops. "No, he didn't. Well, he didn't really have the chance. We've been . . .'"

"I see."

There's a rather long pause.

"We'll do that."

Sheri stares at me, eyes wide. Both Dad and Brittany Anne follow suit.

"Of course. Thank you so much for calling."

When she hangs up, she puts her hands on her hips, like the big red hen in the second-grade spring play. A red hen wearing vagina flowers.

"A concussion! What were you thinking? That was the

teacher from your ski trip. She says you're to go straight to bed."

She turns to Dad. "We have to check on him in the middle of the night and make sure he's responsive."

Please God, do not let Sheri check on me in the middle of the night.

Dad actually looks concerned. "You shoulda said something."

"You were distracted."

"You seen a doctor?" he asks.

"They checked me out at the ski hill. Said I might have a headache for a while."

"Do you want to lie down?"

Well, yes. That was what I was going to do, Dad, before you dumped a kid and a marriage proposal on me. I was going to lie down for a week or so, and now I think I might make it a month. Or longer. I might lie down until next September.

"That would be a good idea."

A celebration dinner: saffron rice, spiced meatballs, and some sort of unidentifiable greens. I watch Brittany Anne eat. She picks all the raisins from the rice and builds them into a pyramid on the side of her plate. Then she eats the rice. Then she eats the pyramid, brick by brick.

This is what Lauren and I could have. This sort of living, breathing creature in our lives. In some ways, the whole idea seems fascinating. And in other ways, it seems so scary that I want to push back from the table right now and sprint for the highway.

Sheri reveals plum cake for dessert. It's nowhere near as delicious as Mom's, which makes me happy.

After dinner and after my dad and I have done the dishes—"only fair after the girls have cooked all day," he says in a cheerful voice I'm no longer used to hearing—Brittany Anne and I play a two-hour game of Monopoly. She cheats, but I let her, because as long as we're playing, I can pretend to be completely absorbed in the game and ignore Sheri and Dad nuzzling each other on the living room couch.

Nausea can be a side effect of a concussion. They warned me about it.

Brittany Anne is surprisingly bright.

"You should change your name to Britt," I tell her. "It sounds less like a s-soap opera star." I was going to say "stripper," but that seemed a bit harsh.

"Do you like Britt better?" she asks.

"Yeah."

"Okay," she says. Then she yells into the living room, "My name is Britt now!"

I can't help smiling, and she responds with an ear-to-ear grin that would get her on one of those reality TV beauty pageant shows. Actually, that would be right up Sheri's alley.

"You shouldn't change your name," Britt says.

"No?"

"I like it."

I have to admit, the girl is growing on me. She's a little ion-powered whirlwind that's sucked all the stale air out of the house.

This doesn't mean I'm okay with her moving in permanently. Not if she wants to bring her mother with her.

At least with Sheri in the house, I'm more motivated to hang out in my bedroom and finish my film. It definitely turned out dark—and I don't mean the background lighting. If this were to hit theaters, researchers would flock to Webster to investigate the population's hopeless, helpless existence. Even to me, the film seems bleak.

It's done, though. Today, I even packaged it up, ready to drop in the mail with my reference letters and my application forms. Since there's going to be a baby in my life, I'll probably never get to film school. But I've spent too much time on the short not to submit it. This way, I can spend the next few years knowing whether or not the studio would have accepted me.

In a sad way, I'm feeling quite confident about it. The film is stark, sure, but they must be used to that at a film school. The whole thing has a rough, raw edge to it. Somehow I'm sure I'll get in, and then I won't be able to go. . . .

I'm thinking about this crazy situation as I search through the linen closet for a sheet to turn into a toga. Lex came through for me, miraculously. She called to say she's convinced Lauren to come to Dallas's party.

Lauren will be there, and I'll be there, and Lex will help arrange a way for us to talk. My chest feels tight even thinking about it. This is a conversation that's going to shape my entire life, Lauren's life, and the baby's.

We're going to make what will probably be our biggest decision ever. While dressed in togas.

"Cole!" There are a dozen people on Dallas's deck who shout my name as I arrive. The bass is pounding. The crowd is a sea of white, although some of the girls dancing outside are wearing ski jackets over their togas.

Both Sheri and Britt ended up helping with my costume, which means my toga has a belt of grape vines. I also have a laurel crown, which I left in the truck so I don't get beat up for looking a whole other level of ridiculous.

"It's freezing out here," I yell.

"It's like a sauna inside," Dallas shouts back. "We go in there to warm up, then out here to cool down. It's like the Swedish-Roman system of good health, bro."

"How's your arm?" I ask him.

"Healing. How's your head? I heard you cracked it open on the ski trip."

"No pink elephants, but I'm still having hallucinations," I say.

"Nice."

"Instead, there's a small child and a stripper living in my house."

"That's awesome!"

The older you get, the more surreal everything becomes. *It's possible that this is how life works,* I think as I shoulder my way inside in search of warmth.

Another example: Across the room from me, Hannah is wearing a toga made from a red satin sheet. She's dancing on top of the kitchen table, which would be surreal even if Lauren weren't dancing on a kitchen chair beside her, wearing an ankle-length toga skirt with a ski jacket zipped up over top. *Inside* the sauna house. Lex is on the floor below them, dancing with both arms in the air and her head bobbing at whiplash-inducing speed.

As I watch, Hannah slips off the table and is caught like a rock concert bodysurfer by the guys conveniently admiring her red satin. She pops back up and keeps dancing. She's like the sexy foil to Lauren's blond angel. Except . . . not so angelic.

It's enough to make you wonder if Salvador Dalí ever hit his head while on a ski trip.

There's a whole field of surrealist documentary filmmaking

that blends fiction and fact. It started when Robert Flaherty fiddled with reality in *Nanook of the North*, and it developed into all sorts of craziness. If I wanted to join that particular stream of filmmaking, this party would be the place to start.

Greg comes in. He nods to me as he makes his way through the kitchen to the cooler of beer.

"How's it going?" I shout.

"Okay." An answer worthy of a sulking woman. I would tell him as much, but he's already squeezed past me again, toward the stereo.

I'm not about to agree with my dead mother's theories of friendship, but parties where no one is speaking to you are less fun than you would think. Lauren's still dancing on the chair, so our Lex-engineered talk is not going to happen anytime soon. Bracing for the cold, I head back to the deck, where Dallas— now wearing a cowboy hat with his toga—appears to be demonstrating a line dance. Only Dallas could get away with that.

I lean on the porch railing, freezing, and wish I had somewhere more comfortable to go. And not just the choice between the heat inside and the cold outside. It's the choice between (a) this party with a bunch of drunk people and (b) the building that used to be my home, a place that suddenly has whole milk instead of skim in the fridge. Sheri says Britt's underweight, and she's supposed to drink the full-fat version.

Whole milk is disgusting.

As Dallas and his followers step-cross-step away from me, I decide another thing's gone wrong with my world. Everything in Webster was supposed to stay the same when I take off for Vancouver. That's how I assumed it would work. People were supposed to wait for me so that when I breezed into town to give my this-is-my-birthplace tour to entertainment news shows, they could be suitably impressed.

But no. They all have their own shit going on. Plans or lack of plans. Babies or stripper families. Brand-new video game systems or roast chicken dinners or lesbian romances.

Most of these people don't even know I'm in a life-altering crisis here. But if they don't understand that, and I don't know what predicaments they might be facing, then something's just not right. And I have a heavy feeling weighing in my gut, telling me it might all be my fault.

chapter 27

surrealism on a whole new level

When I make it inside again, Hannah and Lauren have disappeared from the kitchen table and there's a commotion just down the hallway at the bathroom door. A bunch of drunken girls are pressing into the room as if they're playing sardines, that hide-and-seek game that Greg and I used to like when we were kids.

"Oh my God," one of them shrieks.

"We should call someone." That's Hannah's voice, surprisingly clear.

"She can't stay here."

If I had to guess, I would say some girl's boyfriend got drunk and kissed another girl, which caused the first girl to slap the second girl, ruining her eye makeup, and now all the girls are crying.

That's what I would guess if I had to, but I don't bother. I'm not exactly concerned. At a house party, girls crying in the bathroom is common background noise. I decide to crack a beer and plant my ass on the kitchen counter until Lex signals me. Then I'm going to talk—really talk—to Lauren.

That's my plan—until Lex pushes her way into the kitchen. There's a streak of red down the front of her toga that's definitely more horror movie than surrealist doc.

"There's something wrong with Lauren and the baby," she announces to the room.

"What baby?" someone beside me asks. "Who brought a baby to the party?"

Meanwhile, I've slid from the counter and I'm standing in this weird hyper-alert position, ready to run in whatever direction Lex points. "What do you need?"

It's like she doesn't even see me. Lex spins around with a finger extended and aims it at a random guy.

"You. You gotta call an ambulance," she says.

"Okay," he says, amused. With her mascara smeared and her toga about to fall off her shoulder, Lex is a portrait of a drunken lunatic. *This* is the person I trusted to broker my future with Lauren?

Sucking in air through her teeth, she draws herself up to her full height—somewhere around the guy's belly button—and stabs her finger at him again.

"The ambulance!" she shouts.

"Ambulance. Got it." He doesn't move.

I'm patting my pockets for my own phone, but it must be in the truck. I can't see a house phone through the crowd. And then all hell breaks loose. More people try to jam themselves into the bathroom. Someone starts screaming for help, and everyone on the deck attempts to press inside.

I don't know what I'm supposed to do. It's as if I'm caught in one of those melodramatic silent films, in which some girl is tied to the railway tracks and everyone is running this way and that. Except in this case, Lauren is stuck in the bathroom and Lex is trying to punch the guy across from me. He's blocking her blows and her mouth is still moving, lips flapping in exaggerated motions, though no sound is reaching my ears except friggin' Charlie Chaplin music until finally—finally—Hannah steps into the center of things.

"Cole!" Her voice snaps like a whip. This is not the dancing-on-a-kitchen-table Hannah. She is undeniably sober. "I can't get them out of the bathroom."

I nod.

"Cole! You need to get these girls out of the bathroom. Can you do that?"

Clear the bathroom. I take a breath, and wonder how long I've been holding the same air in my lungs. *Breathe. Get them out of the bathroom. I can do that.*

Maybe they're wrong about Lauren. Maybe it's indigestion.

As soon as Hannah's out of the way, I take Lex by the shoulders and physically lift her to the side. As I move the few steps down the hallway to the bathroom, I do the same to another dozen girls. I'm a bulldozer removing boulders. Eventually, I clear my way to Lauren, who is sitting on the vinyl floor staring at the blood on her toga. Her skin is the same color as the sheet, which seems eerily impossible. Her entire body is shaking.

This is not indigestion.

Is there supposed to be this much blood when you have a baby?

Lauren looks at me as if I'm a knight who will save her, but my brain is threatening to shut down again. I can feel my heart beating. The human heart is not supposed to beat this fast.

Behind me, the word "pregnant" ripples from mouth to mouth in a sound wave traveling away from the bathroom.

"Cole?" Lauren says. I sink to my knees beside her, not sure where it's safe to touch her.

"Can you get me out of here?" she asks.

Outside, the stereo stops. I hear Hannah shouting instructions. "Everybody out! The party's over. Greg, call an ambulance. Dallas, get the fucking hat off your head and turn on some lights in here. Somebody give me a cell phone."

Behind us, girls are pressing into the bathroom again. The pressure's building like the weight of snow on a mountain cliff, ready to bury us.

Lauren is still staring up at me, skin damp, eyes wide and scared.

I move to a squat, snaking an arm under her shoulders and another beneath her legs. "Had enough of this party?"

When she nods, I scoop her up in my arms, then shoulder my way out of the bathroom. Once I'm in motion, my brain seems to work. Maybe that's the trick to crisis management. Stay in motion.

"Cole, I haven't talked to her yet! Stay away!" Lex screams at me. I refuse to break focus.

The kitchen is crammed with people and the deck is no better, so I carry Lauren all the way to the driveway.

"The ambulance is on its way," Hannah says, following us.

A wave of people pours out of the house and gathers around, pushing close. Some of the girls are crying; they all seem to be yelling.

Lauren grows heavy in my arms but I can't exactly lay her on the snow or the gravel.

Lex is here too, shrill and insistent.

"Leave her alone, Cole Owens!"

Lex seems to think she's supposed to be between us. When I don't respond, she swings her purse at my head, and then she actually starts kicking me. Kicking me! The girl's wearing high-heeled boots.

Eventually, I manage to get the door of my truck open and settle Lauren on the passenger seat.

"You can't take her!" Lex screams. She has backup now—a gang of drunk girls who echo everything she says.

As Lex winds up to kick me again, I consider grabbing her foot. But what would that accomplish? It wouldn't get help for Lauren any faster. I can hear a siren growing closer, so I angle the truck's passenger door between my legs and Lex's boot, and I put my jacket over Lauren.

"I think I'm dying," Lauren whimpers.

"You're not dying," I tell her. "The ambulance is coming. Can you hear it?"

"If I'm not dying, my parents are going to kill me," she says.

I consider this. "It's possible. But only after they kill me."

A fire truck is the first to arrive, and an ambulance squeals up behind. Flashing emergency lights paint the masses red, then blue, as if we're all at some alien dance club. The sight of men in uniforms finally makes everyone back up. The crowd grows quiet.

It's only me and Hannah and Lex standing by the truck when the men drop red bags and a stretcher beside us. Lex is still ranting, but I'm concentrating on the deep voice of the paramedic. It's like Valium, slowing everything.

"So what happened here?" he asks.

"She needs a hospital," I blurt.

"She's pregnant," Hannah says. I wince at the word. "She was bleeding all day and didn't tell anyone and then she was drinking, and she fell, and . . ."

How does Hannah know all of this? It's as if my ex-girlfriends have formed a secret society behind my back.

A crying Lex interjects something unintelligible, and a second paramedic puts a hand on her shoulder to calm her. There is stuff streaming from Lex's nose the way little kids on rainy days have unnoticed snot.

The paramedics examine Lauren, calling numbers to each other. Then, like choreographed dancers, they step away from the truck and whisk a stretcher into place, lifting Lauren onto it like a life-size practice doll.

My brain must be in shock again because as Lauren's loaded into the ambulance, I find myself thinking that the stretcher is a cool invention. It wheels out, the legs unfold to the exact height of my truck, then fold back up to be slid into the ambulance. While I'm pondering the mysteries of hydraulics, Lex climbs in beside the paramedic and sits by Lauren like a watch-dog, as if she rides in ambulances every weekend. As if she's Lauren's best friend.

I try to join them, but the paramedic reaches out and puts a hand on my chest.

"You been drinking?" he asks.

I shake my head. I never got to drink that beer I popped.

"Follow us, then. Use the ER entrance."

Then the ambulance doors close in my face like theater curtains and I can't help worrying that "The End" has appeared in scrolled letters.

Cursing, I race back to my truck and climb in, revving the engine to clear the bystanders from behind me. I'm about to rip backward when the passenger door opens and Hannah climbs in.

"What the . . . ?" I'm supposed to follow my pregnant ex-girlfriend to the hospital with my other ex-girlfriend in the truck beside me? I open my mouth, but I have no idea what to say.

Hannah, apparently, has no shortage of words. "I was going to make her see you. I swear. We've been talking a lot in the last couple weeks. I thought it was completely unfair of her to shut you out. She said she'd talk to you tonight. But then it was crazy in there, and when I saw you . . ."

I have this urge to wrap my arms around Hannah. I want to rest my forehead right in that dip above her collarbone. . . .

No.

The ambulance is out of the driveway, turning onto the main road. Right now, I have to follow Lauren.

I reach for the gearshift, and the truck door whips open. Again.

"Move over."

There are very few people who would argue with Greg when he sounds like that. Without a word, Hannah slides onto the console, and Greg climbs in beside her.

"What are you thinking?" he says to me. "Go!"

And with a spray of gravel, I floor it.

Again, I'm remembering the time Lauren called me to her house and I found her curled on the couch, a pillow pressed against her stomach. She was trying to tell me something until she noticed Hannah idling outside.

"Fuck."

"That's how it usually happens," Greg says. His head has rolled back against the headrest and his eyes are closed. "I told you months ago that something was wrong with her."

"I know," I say.

"You knew?" Hannah asks Greg.

"Only since Cole announced that she didn't have a thyroid problem."

"I know," I say again, before either of them can tell me how stupid I am.

That lunch hour in the school foyer, discussing Lauren's disintegrating fashion sense and Greg's dating plans—the whole scene rotates around me. The giggling girls. The posse surrounding Lauren. The guy trying to jump onto the snack stand counter. Greg sitting beside me, tenting his fingers and working up the courage to tell me he wants to date Lauren.

But this entire scene *wasn't* rotating around me. All the big things were happening to other people. I was just a bystander. Just the guy behind the camera. A scrap of space junk in a universe of shit.

"Sorry."

Greg snorts. "You so completely do not deserve that girl," he says flatly.

Hannah says nothing, but I feel her shoulders curl inward.

I'm about to agree. I don't deserve Lauren. Or Hannah. Or Greg either, for that matter. But then we're at the hospital. We fling ourselves out of the truck and all three of us run—run—across the parking lot, our togas flapping behind us like surrender flags.

chapter 28

hospitals smell like lysol, pee, and death

"We're here for Lauren Michaels," Greg says to the woman at the desk, who looks entirely uninterested in emergencies.

"Have a seat." She waves vaguely to the waiting room chairs without looking up.

We move in unison across the room, pulled together somehow by her indifference.

"Did someone call Lauren's mom?" I wonder as we drop into the orange plastic chairs.

As if in answer, the glass doors sweep open and Lauren's parents race into the room with a blast of cold air. Her dad goes straight to the desk. Her mom sees us as we jump up from our seats, and she stops.

"They took her inside," Greg says.

"I didn't know, until . . . ," I blurt, much less helpfully. I can't help feeling like there's accusation in Mrs. Michaels's eyes.

She doesn't respond. Maybe she doesn't even know what I'm talking about. Her husband says her name, and they both half-jog past the desk and down the hallway. Greg, Hannah, and I flop back down.

We wait. Hannah takes my hand, which is more helpful and less uncomfortable than I would have thought. A few more of Lauren's friends show up and perch, sniffling softly, on the other side of the waiting room. A man in green hospital scrubs sweeps through from outside, his hair sticking up as if he was called out of bed. He too disappears down the hallway.

We wait.

Greg calls his mom and I listen as he summarizes the events. I consider calling my dad, but I wouldn't know how to start explaining this particular situation.

Hannah goes to find a bathroom, leaving Greg and me side by side.

"I messed up," I say, staring at the scuffed floor.

"Yeah. You two will work it out, though."

"No. I mean, yes, I messed up with Lauren. But I messed things up with you too."

Greg just grunts.

"You're a better friend than me." Some people have a talent for that. For turning up exactly when you need them and being exactly what you need. I'm not one of those people.

Hannah sits down again.

After a while, my butt seems permanently molded to the plastic chair.

The door from the parking lot slides open, and everyone in the waiting room looks up expectantly. It's Greg's mom. She hands us each a pair of pants and a T-shirt. Once we've pulled them on and ditched the sheets, she drops into the seat beside Greg, her shoulder against his. She sits there without saying anything. For the first time since elementary school, I find myself loving Greg's mom.

We wait.

This time, it's the clicking sound of high heels that makes our heads snap to attention. Lex emerges from the ER, looking as if she was pulled behind the ambulance instead of allowed to ride inside.

"She's okay so far," she says. "They say she lost a lot of blood, but she's stopped hemorrhaging for now."

My jaw relaxes a little, and I wonder how long it's been clenched. Maybe since Dallas's house.

"What about the . . . ?" one of the girls asks from across the room.

"We don't know yet." Lex doesn't look at me. No one looks at me.

Finally, I can't stand it anymore. This is not a sit-in-the-waiting-room sort of situation. I get up and walk toward the swinging doors that divide us from the ER.

"Only family members allowed," the woman behind the desk says.

"I'm the father of the baby." The word "father" falls like a brick off my tongue, but at least it gets me past the desk. In the row of green-sheeted compartments, I find Lauren lying on a hospital bed, face turned slightly away from where her mom stands gripping Lauren's dad's arm.

Mrs. Michaels glares at me. There's no question this time. She knows.

"I'd like to talk to Cole," Lauren says. Her skin is still frighteningly pale, but she doesn't sound as scared anymore.

When her mom sniffs, Lauren turns to look her in the eye. Her mom glances away. Mr. Michaels pats his wife's arm and avoids looking at his daughter.

The two of them squeeze by me, stiff like icicles, careful to ensure their clothes don't brush against mine in the narrow opening between fabric walls.

Once they're a few steps away, I perch on the edge of the bed. There are no chairs in this enclosure, only machines.

"I should have talked to you earlier," Lauren says.

"I should have figured things out months ago."

"You were already with Hannah. . . ."

"What did they say? The doctors?"

Lauren bites her lip. "Nothing yet. The doctor came and left. The nurses did an exam. They said the bleeding's stopped. Someone's supposed to come and talk to me."

I take her hand.

I'm not used to the hospital being this quiet. For once, there's no old lady groaning in pain, no loud, beeping machines, no crazy man yelling from the hallway about his bowel movements. There's only the efficient slap of the nurses' shoes as they pass back and forth. Red numbers blink at me from the terminal beside the IV stand, and fluid drip, drip, drips down the plastic tubing into Lauren's arm. I hold her palm lightly, rubbing my thumb across it. Mostly to reassure myself.

In the week before my mother died, her skin loosened itself, bagging under her eyes and folding itself down her neck like a balloon with the helium seeping away. Before that, Mom would sometimes look tired or pained or angry. In those last few days, she started to look . . . absent. I didn't ask the nurses about it, not even Tracy or the once-a-day doctor on his hurried rounds, because I didn't want to hear their answers, and I didn't want Mom to hear them either. Dad and I stopped talking too. It was the end of August. I went to the hospital every lunch hour and every afternoon. Dad would go early every morning before work and late each night. We barely saw each other. Sometimes we left notes to each other on the table with Mom's portions of hospital food. Unread notes tucked underneath trays of uneaten food.

"What am I going to do, Cole?" Lauren whispers. The question's a few months too late, but I don't say that.

"We'll figure it out," I reassure her. "We can get a place, if you want. Or we can stay at my place, although it's a little more crowded than usual at the moment. My dad's girlfriend moved in, with her daughter."

Lauren looks surprised, and her eyebrows go even higher at the end. I don't explain. I'm busy feeling dreams pop, like soap bubbles: my Vancouver apartment, actresses fawning over me, coffee shops, martini bars, film school. Film school.

It hurts, as each one disappears. It hurts less than I would have expected, though. As I stare at Lauren's eyelashes, translucent against her skin, I imagine a baby—an actual baby—with those lashes. Turning the word "father" over in my head, I remember what my subconscious was trying to tell me while I was stuck in that tree well, about friends being safety nets.

I think about what Dallas said: You don't go to the bar and then scoot your ass out when the fight starts.

All this time, I've been thinking of the Web as a trap. Maybe it's a safety net. All those tangled relationships—they keep you stuck in one place, but they also keep you together. Web. Net. Are those the same thing?

"We'll figure it out," I say again.

There's a loud throat clearing behind me and a nurse nods at both of us. Lauren's parents are back, peering over the nurse's shoulder.

I stand and inch back against the curtain.

"Do they know what's happening?" Lauren asks as the nurse slides a blood pressure cuff onto her arm.

"The doctor will be here in a little while," the nurse says, her eyes focused on the equipment.

Another throat clearing. Lauren's dad this time.

"Cole? Can you come back in a few minutes?" Lauren says.

I'm released back into the hallway, but I don't go through the swinging doors. I hover at the edge of the ER.

Here's another soft-focus scene, slightly overexposed from the light bouncing off the all-white walls.

One afternoon in the hospital, Mom looked at me with her eyes a little brighter blue than they had been, and she asked me to find her a specific story.

"It's in one of my old textbooks," she said. "A little girl is sick and she's supposed to die before the last leaf falls off the vine by her bedroom window."

"Mom!" I protested. "What kind of story is that?"

"No, she doesn't die. Someone . . . her grandfather, maybe, or her neighbor . . . I don't remember; someone paints a leaf on the wall by the vine so it never falls."

Mom closed her eyes a few minutes later. Even that much talking was enough to tire her. I got up to go, barely kissing her cheek so I wouldn't wake her.

"Cole?" she asked just as I was in the doorway. "You'll be okay?"

I nodded, my throat closing up in that way that I hated.

I never did find the story about the leaf. Later that night a nurse called from the hospital and woke Dad and me. We picked up two separate phone extensions simultaneously.

"Her pulse ox is pretty low," the nurse said. "You should probably be here."

Within minutes, we were in the truck, shivering from the damp cold and driving through darkened streets without another car in sight. We didn't say a single word to each other.

By the time we got there, a nurse was already disconnecting Mom's wires.

"She left?" my dad said, disbelieving. Taking Mom's hand from the sheet, he leaned down and pressed it to his forehead.

The nurse bustled a chair behind him, but he didn't sit. He stayed bent in half, like a broken tree.

"She left," he repeated. He didn't say, "She's gone."

I knew exactly what he meant.

I'm standing in the middle of the hallway when a pair of arms wrap around me.

"I came as soon as I heard." It's Tracy, and I swear I've never been so happy to see a pierced lip in my entire life. She knows Lauren, of course. We spent enough lunch hours here together last year. I let myself rest my head on Tracy's shoulder, just for a second.

"I don't know what's going on," I tell her.

She tilts her head down the hall, and I follow her to a little row of chairs lined against one wall.

"She's pregnant," I tell her. "Someone said she was bleeding all day. And she was bleeding at the party. . . ."

Tracy nods. I guess she knows all this already.

"Her mom doesn't want me in there with her, and I don't know what's happening."

"The doctor's going to talk to Lauren," she says. "He and I just spoke."

"What? What did he say?"

Tracy sighs. "Cole," she says. "There was a lot of blood. She could bleed again at any time. And her cervix is open."

I don't really know what this means.

"She's far enough along that there was a small chance that a baby could survive. But there was no heartbeat."

In Tracy's eyes, I find the meaning of those words. She takes my hand and squeezes it as the significance sinks in.

"There's no baby," I say finally.

"Not anymore. She'll have to have surgery, something called a D and C, to remove the tissue and the placenta. They're waiting for the anesthetist to arrive."

Another bubble pops, just like the film school bubble popped a little while ago. Strangely, this one hurts more.

"She doesn't know yet?"

"Only the doctor's supposed to tell her," Tracy says.

I have to tell her. We're in this together now. I can't let her hear the news from a stranger, without me there.

I'm surprisingly calm. I'm breathing normally. My heart rate is steady. I notice these things with one half of my brain. The other half only registers that my guts have been scraped out with a spoon. Inside, I'm all raw wounds. A big bloody mess.

And yet, I thank Tracy, my voice solid. Then I clear my throat at the door of the cubicle. Her parents and I perform the same sheet-doorway dance for a third time.

I sit on the bed beside Lauren, my hip touching hers. "I

talked to a nurse," I say. I don't use Tracy's name. I don't want to get her in trouble if this gets repeated later.

Lauren surprises me.

"The baby's gone," she whispers.

I nod, and then she's crying. Her arms are around my shoulders, tubing everywhere, and she's shaking with sobs, crying like a little girl. I cry too, partly for Lauren and partly for me and partly because of what used to be a baby, a small human being. Gone. The images flashing through my head are all mixed up. There's my mom, lying on hospital sheets like the ones on this bed. There's Lauren on the bathroom floor, pale and bloody. There's even the damn dead deer, side heaving on the highway.

"You always teased me for wanting to stay in Webster," Lauren says after a long while.

"I didn't mean . . ."

"No, it's okay. I just want you to know, I didn't want to stay like this. This isn't how I planned things. I didn't want to be the girl who didn't finish high school."

"It doesn't mean we wouldn't have taken care of a baby."

She nods. "I think I knew it was gone, Cole. I think it's been gone for a while."

After that, we're quiet for a long time. I guess we don't need to explain to each other this mix of sadness and confusion and, though it feels wrong, relief.

"I should tell my mom," she says eventually.

"Do you want me to stay?"

She shakes her head. "No. If Lex is calm, you can send her in after a bit."

"Cole?" Lauren calls me back as I turn to leave. "Thanks for telling me. And thanks for offering. To stay with me."

I nod. I did offer, didn't I? I offered to stay and be a decent dad. I stayed between these curtains with her and shared the pain of our whole messed-up situation. And even though I caused this pregnancy in the first place, I was also part of the safety net. I feel a tiny, amoeba-size bit better.

Back in the waiting room, everyone stands as I enter. All of them. Greg and Greg's mom, Hannah, and Lex, and the girl posse. Even Ms. Gladwell and my dad, who have somehow arrived too. You can't escape anyone in this town.

They're all staring at me, waiting.

"She lost the baby," I say. The entire room exhales.

I turn toward Lex. "Have you got it together?"

She glares at me as if she's never had an un-together moment. I glance at Hannah, who nods that Lex is okay.

"Lauren is asking for you."

"Are you all right?" Ms. Gladwell asks me. At the same time, my dad puts a cup of vending machine coffee in my hand.

I nod. I'm as all right as I can be under the circumstances. Not quite ready to deal with these two yet, though. Not ready to analyze my feelings for Ms. Gladwell or make light of them for my dad. Not ready to wonder how you can lose a baby so soon after you've discovered its existence.

I step up to the sensor and the doors swoosh open, releasing me into the cold. The air sears my lungs, but it doesn't stop the tears rolling down my face. Suddenly, what I want most in the world is to talk to my mom. Even my imaginary mom would do. I'd take a hallucination.

The lights in the houses across the road are dark. There's only the streetlight shining down on the corner church with its marquee board.

I AM WITH YOU ALWAYS, EVEN UNTO THE END OF THE WORLD.

It seems less like a threat this time and more like a message. Maybe from God, or maybe from my mom. Looking at that sign makes me feel a little better.

Behind me, the door opens again. Greg and Hannah emerge, their shoulders hunched against the wind.

I'm happy to see them. I turn that over in my head for a minute, just to make sure the feeling's real.

It is. I'm happy to see them.

"I'm going for a walk," I say. "You want to come?"

And even though it's the middle of the night and pretty much the Arctic outside, they both say yes. It's hard to come by friends like that. Or so says my dead mother.

If this were a film, there would be a real ending. Something solid to point to and say "final scene." In a documentary like *Hoop Dreams*, I'd be the basketball player who failed to make it big. I would have told Lauren we would care for the baby together, my film school dream would have popped like a bubble, and I would be left here in obscurity. Or maybe I'm one of the kids who failed to win the good-school lottery in *Waiting for Superman*. But there's no baby anymore. School *is* waiting, as is the promise of success.

This night doesn't seem entirely tragic or entirely happy. Not even close.

Seems like life doesn't have a documentary ending. In fact, it's possible that my bleak film, bundled into its manila envelope, has entirely the wrong conclusion. It turns out that Webster isn't necessarily the problem and escaping isn't the answer. In reality, things are messier.

"I'm sorry, to both of you," I tell Hannah and Greg. "I've been an ass."

Neither disagrees. I reach for Hannah's hand and enclose it in mine.

"I should have realized how great you two are."

"You're not so bad yourself," Greg says.

The relief that surges through me is so strong that I have to squeeze my eyes shut for a minute until I can breathe.

"You could have talked to us," Hannah says.

"That too."

We walk, in the dark, until Hannah's lips are blue and everyone's teeth are chattering and it's time to check on Lauren again. Time to face the room.

chapter 29

the screening

The surgery's over. Lauren's asleep on her hospital bed, her mom sitting vigil beside her. She was right about the baby being gone for a while. That's what Tracy said.

Once Ms. Gladwell has gone home and Greg's mom has given my dad a ride back to the house, Greg and Hannah are still with me. We huddle over paper cups of hot chocolate, in a corner of the waiting room that we seem to have claimed as our own.

"You want to go on a Vancouver road trip with me next summer, help me rent an apartment?" I ask Greg.

He doesn't answer right away. Maybe he hasn't entirely forgiven me.

"You can decide later, I guess."

He shakes his head. "I was just thinking maybe you want to rent a two-bedroom place. I'm going to sign up for an apprenticeship program there."

This makes me sit up straight. "Seriously?"

"Yeah. I can work for my dad during the summers. He thinks it's a good idea."

I look over at Hannah, and she's smiling.

"We can make it the three of us, if you want. Like a commune. We can all eat quinoa and make our own yogurt so it feels like home to Greg," I say.

That makes Hannah roll her eyes. "Personally, I'll stick to a dorm room," she says. "But thanks."

"I'll take the commune," Greg says. "But not the quinoa. And, Hannah, the doors are always open. You know what happens in communes. They like to share. Everything."

She actually laughs, loud enough to make the reception desk nurse stare in our direction.

"Leave me out of it. We could hang out sometimes, though. See some films," she says, looking at me.

"That would be good." Her leg brushes against mine, tentative. I shift toward her slightly so our knees touch.

"What about Lauren?" Greg asks.

"I don't think she wants to live in our commune either," I say.

"Very funny."

I take a good look at him. His hands wrap around the paper cup. They're huge and creased with auto grease. They're grown-up hands.

"I don't think she wants to marry me and live behind a white picket fence anymore," I tell him. "And even if she did, her mother would murder me. Or Lex would."

"Lex is a nightmare," Greg agrees.

"Are you kidding?" Hannah says. "She stuck up for Lauren this whole time. And she was the only one Lauren trusted with the truth."

We're silent for a minute, considering this.

"I still think Lauren has room for new friends in her life," I venture.

Greg nods thoughtfully.

"Why don't you check on her?" I say. "Maybe she's awake."

"You think?"

Hannah leans her head on my shoulder as we watch Greg walk past the desk. It feels weird to have him checking on my ex, but it doesn't feel wrong. Not anymore. He loves her. Maybe he's loved her since second grade, in different ways at different times, just as I have. It seems like this whole hospital is a tangle of friends and ex-girlfriends and teachers and parents, wound together, all waiting to care for whichever one of us breaks down next.

The idea doesn't seem as suffocating as it used to.

Actually, I'm kinda grateful.

Eventually, we all go home. I drop Greg off at his orange and stucco house, where his mom is waiting at the kitchen window. I drop Hannah at her mansion. The porch light is on, and when I pull into the driveway, her dad steps outside. He nods at me before he wraps his daughter in his arms.

Then I take myself home. The lights are on there too. It seems as if our families have been awake all night, waiting for us.

"You all right?" Dad asks from the recliner in the basement.

"Yeah."

"Get some sleep," he says.

And when I go into my room, my sheets are turned down, the same way my mom used to do when I was a kid. Which makes me wonder if it was my mom after all. Do dads turn down sheets? Then, as my head sinks into the pillow, I smell the faintest trace of gardenias. And it doesn't even matter. It still feels like I'm home.

Five days later, I stare at my computer screen, drumming my fingers on the desk, while Britt jumps on the recliner.

"Is it ready yet?" she calls.

"Almost!"

Whenever I blink, I feel grit behind my eyelids. I haven't slept much. The morning after I got home from the hospital, the first thing I did was rip open my film school application package. I've been reediting ever since.

It's almost finished. Not quite, but almost. Today, Hannah, Greg, Dallas, and even Tracy and Ms. Gladwell are coming over for an advance screening. Hannah's already here, helping Sheri choose paint colors for the baby's room. Lauren's stuck at home. She's not allowed out of bed for a few more days, but I've promised to bring her a finished version.

A shadow falls across my keyboard. I glance up to see my dad, his bulk filling the doorway.

"Almost done," I tell him. "I'll bring it upstairs."

"It's not that," he says. "I just wanted to say hello. See how you're doing."

Since when does my dad stop by to chat? There's so much we haven't said, and so many things I haven't explained, it seems impossible to start now.

"I'm kinda busy," I say. Although really, all I have to do now is watch the progress bar slide across the screen as the DVD burns.

Dad doesn't take the hint. He comes right into my room and sits on the bed. "I know things haven't been so great over the past year."

I nod. Understatement's a beautiful thing.

"I guess I wasn't always . . . here. For you. You know what I mean?" he asks.

Suddenly I have an image of us in a Clint Eastwood western, decked out in leather holsters, facing each other across a dusty street.

"It's fine," I say.

"Now that Sheri's here . . ." Dad trails off.

I look up. Is Sheri going to solve everything? Is that what he's come here to say? A few months ago, the idea would have filled me with rage. Now it just seems absurd. I want to grab him by the shoulders and say, "Look, we messed up. You screwed up, and I screwed up. Literally. Let's just put away the guns and walk our separate ways."

In those westerns, they don't blab on about their deep inner emotions. It's fairly simple. If they like each other, they tip their hats. If they dislike each other, they shoot.

"Things are going to get better," Dad says. "She's not your mom. I know that. Your mom, she was one of a kind."

His voice cracks on that last word. Which is probably why gunslingers stick to tipping their hats. I find myself blinking, hard, as I stare at the progress bar.

"She'd be real proud of you."

I snort. I can't help it. "Yeah, as I run around getting into bar fights and impregnating girls. I'm sure she'd be real proud."

"Girls?" Dad asks. "There aren't any others, are there?"

"Figure of speech. There was only Lauren."

"Well, I'm just saying, your mom'd be proud. You've handled things real well."

Something inside me softens. It's like he's walked three-quarters across the dusty street to meet me. I could at least step off the boardwalk.

"I think you're right about things getting better," I say. "And Sheri? She's okay. I like Britt."

"They're both good people, Cole. They're happy to have us too," he says.

He has a good smile, one that makes his eyes look brighter. I haven't seen him smile much, not for a long time.

I shake my head. You think as your world is heading to hell, some people are going to hold it together. The ones who are older than you, and bigger than you, and presumably smarter than you. When they climb into the handbasket too, it's seriously concerning. Who would have thought that a pregnant stripper would be the one to get my dad back on his feet?

Not even Hollywood could invent this stuff.

As Dad gets up from the bed, Britt barrels into the room.

"Aren't you ready yet?"

"Two minutes!"

The doorbell rings, and she runs for it. Dad follows more slowly.

"A documentary, eh?" he says from the doorway.

"Yeah."

"I always did like movies about real stuff. There's no glitzing things up."

Then he leaves, before I can agree.

Voices echo from the entranceway—Greg and Dallas. The bell rings again, and more footsteps cross the floor upstairs. I listen to muffled laughter and it feels good. It feels good to have them all here.

With a beep, the disc is finally finished. I grab it and head to the living room.

"And the award for director of the year goes to . . . Cole Owens," Greg says in a deep announcer's voice. Dallas and Britt both cheer. Ms. Gladwell and Tracy smile, and Tracy gives me one of her bear hugs.

"All right, all right. Grab a seat," I say.

I slide the disc into the machine and dim the lights. Butterflies the size of pterodactyls are doing acrobatics in my stomach. Is this how every director feels when people see his film for the first time? When Cameron Crowe screens a film in Cannes, are his palms sweating?

Behind me, Greg, Dallas, and Hannah are squashed together

on the couch. Tracy sits in the recliner and Ms. Gladwell perches on the arm of the chair. Britt sits cross-legged on the floor. My dad and Sheri both hover in the doorway to the kitchen.

The music starts. Then my face fills the screen.

"This is Webster," I say. "It's a tiny place you've never heard of, filled with people you've never met."

The scene changes to a view of Canyon Street, shoppers strolling between the stores.

"Around here," my voice continues, "we call Webster 'the Web.' And I used to think of it as a trap, like a giant spiderweb."

Now the film cuts to Greg, in the darkened truck, asking me to believe him if he sees aliens.

On the couch, Greg groans.

The next scene is him again, in front of the bakery. I've left both our voices in the clip—me, asking if he feels trapped, and him, basically saying he's okay. He's a happy guy in front of a nice bakery.

Dallas is up next, also talking about the town in kind terms.

Then I'm narrating again, over top of a scene at the Burger Barn. I talk about how none of these people describe the Web in the way I expect. They don't seem to understand my idea of showing the irony of the name and the spiderweb nature of the town. "Oh, they admit there are a few problems," I say into the camera. "Not everything's perfect."

Now there's Hannah in the Nester bandstand.

In the living room, Greg lets out a low wolf whistle, and Hannah elbows him.

On-screen, she talks about how hard it is to find your place in a town where people already know each other so well.

Then her face fades, and mine replaces it. "For every new person struggling to fit in, there's another who finds the Web a place of refuge," I narrate. My voice leads into the interview with Tracy, aglow with love and biodynamic blueberries.

And finally, Greg appears for a third time, clarifying his views on aliens and why it's so important that someone believe him.

The film ends with a sweeping view of the valley.

"I was wrong about Webster," says my disembodied voice. "Oh, it's a web. But it's not a trap. Turns out, the tangled nature of this place, where everyone knows everyone and everyone's involved in everybody's business . . . that's what holds us all together."

Back to the close-up of my face. "I still want to leave," I say. "There are other places to see, and I have things I want to accomplish. I can do that knowing Webster is here supporting me. It's like a giant-size safety net, woven from the threads of community."

The credits roll. The whole room breaks into applause.

I am horrified to find tears on my cheeks. To cover, I grab Britt from the floor and toss her into the air a few times.

"Did you like it?" I ask.

"I loved it!" she says. She's not the most critical of critics, but when I risk a glance around the room, it looks as if everyone else loved it too.

"You left out the dead deer," Greg says after he's slapped me on the back a few times.

Hannah stares at him as if he's lost his mind.

"I hated to leave such a great shot unused," I say with a smirk. That dead deer was the final scene of my first edit. There was just no way to include it in the second version—not without taking all the focus away from the living people.

"You guys can help me think of a title," I say. "I was considering *Entangled*."

Hannah shakes her head. "Too Disney."

"Call it *Little Green Men*," Dallas offers.

"Shut up," Greg tells him.

"You know," Sheri says from the kitchen door. "You all got a bond here that a lot of people would love to have. And that web you're talking about, it's important. I think you should call it *Life in the Web*."

This is possibly the first time I've ever heard Sheri say something meaningful. It would be easier to absorb if her hand weren't toying with the nape of my dad's neck. But still . . .

"*Life in the Web*. I like it," Dad says.

The rest of them are nodding too.

As they haul themselves off the couch and the floor and go in search of snacks, Hannah gives me one more hug.

"You did a fantastic job."

"Yeah?"

She nods. "I'm proud to be part of the Web with you."

I smile back at her. For the first time in my life, I'm proud to be part of the Web too. Which is a little ironic since I hope to be leaving in a few months. But maybe . . . maybe you have to know where you come from, and what you are, before you run away to become something new.

I let out a long, slow breath, happy to have this first screening over with and relieved that it went so well. Then I kiss Hannah. I kiss her the way movie stars kiss in the final scene, when they've navigated all the roadblocks that the screenwriter dropped in their paths and they finally understand where they're supposed to be. Then fireworks paint the sky behind them.

"I still have a lot to figure out," I tell her, once we've caught our breath.

"We'll get there," she says.

The next morning, before I slide the disc into the package to send to the admissions office, I watch the film one last time.

I find myself pressing pause as the camera pans through

Burger Barn. The customers sprinkled among the tables, most young, some not, are living their own rom-coms, or action flicks, or family-friendly movies. Maybe one or two are in the midst of some dark, heavy documentary filled with seemingly unsolvable problems. Some of them are probably acting, following scripts and instructions, but maybe a few have realized that they're actually the directors. They're sitting in the chair, making the big decisions.

If I could tweak the focus, see their eyes, maybe I could tell what kind of film they're living. Or maybe not, even then. Sometimes you don't understand what those around you are going through, even if you eat cereal with them every morning or pass by their locker every afternoon.

"Breakfast!" Sheri's voice trills down the stairs.

I hear Britt's pattering steps and Dad's heavy ones. It won't be a normal breakfast. It will be frittata or eggs Florentine or some other dish that takes ridiculous amounts of effort at this hour of the morning. But Dad will sit lapping it up and Sheri will beam at him.

This last day or so, I've felt a flicker. It's as if an old-fashioned projector reel has hummed to life inside me. A week ago, everything seemed to be ending. And now—now I think this might be a new beginning. A new opening scene.

I can guess at what's coming next, but there's no way to

know for sure. And there's no way to know how this film ends or when. Could be a spiderwebbed windshield. Could be a falling leaf, seen from a palliative-care bed on the third floor.

I suppose that's the whole point of being the director. You have to call the shots. If you end up living in Webster with your lesbian lover, or changing the oil on the fifth Ford pickup of the day, or lost in the crowds of some big city—whatever happens, at least know that you chose that scene.

I pop the film into its case just as a honk sounds outside. Hannah's arranged a snowshoeing trip for the day. I have a surprise for her too. A giant-size, specially imported bag of pork rinds. Her life won't be complete until she tries them.

But first, she should come inside for breakfast. We both might like eggs Florentine. After that . . . well, there are still more scenes to be shot.

ACKNOWLEDGMENTS

I am absolutely bubbling over with gratitude for the people who helped me create this book. The BC Arts Council provided financial support. A huge thank-you to my wonderful agent, Patricia Ocampo, and her colleague Marie Campbell at Transatlantic Literary Agency. Thank you also to everyone at Simon & Schuster, especially Annette Pollert, who helped bring Cole to life.

And, of course, I couldn't have written the book without the support of Min, Julia, and Matthew, who put up with a wife/mother who spent long periods having imaginary conversations in her head and neglecting to answer real-life questions. Thank you also to my friend and mentor Colleen MacMillan, and to Gordon, Shirley, and Sandy Lloyd for being willing beta readers, defenders of small towns everywhere, and founts of sage advice.

Nicole Ebert answered all my medical questions (although any mistakes are mine, of course!), and Carl Hofbauer lent me his film lore and lingo. Leanne Lafrance and Gord Bradley solved my life's crises while I wrote, and Arlene Fidel and Liliana Villalpando kept my children alive—thank you for being my village.

Finally, I am blessed and spoiled by the support of two fabulous groups of women. The Inkslingers (Rachelle Delaney, Kallie George, Christy Goerzen, Maryn Quarless, and Lori Sherritt-Fleming) is the best critique group on earth. Every time we meet, I feel honored to be in such company. And the Dirty Girls Running Group Which Doesn't Actually Run (Alex Bayne, Heidi De Lazzer, Jacqui Thomas, Joanna Clark, Shanda Jordan, Krystal Beley, and Rebecca Porte) keeps my world spinning on dark days and bright ones.

Thank you!